KEEPING THE EMBERS ALIVE
MUSICIANS OF ZIMBABWE

Interviews and Commentary by
MYRNA CAPP

Photographs by
KRISTIN CAPP

Drawings by
Teri Capp

Africa World Press, Inc.

P.O. Box 1892
Trenton, NJ 08607

P.O. Box 48
Asmara, ERITREA

Book and cover design: Saverance Publishing Services
                           (www.saverancepublishing.com)

Cover photos: Kristin Capp

Library of Congress Cataloging-in-Publication Data

Capp, Myrna.
 Keeping the embers alive : musicians of Zimbabwe / interviews and commentary by Myrna Capp ; photographs by Kristin Capp ; drawings by Teri Capp.
     p. cm.
 ISBN 1-59221-429-0 (cloth) -- ISBN 1-59221-430-4 (pbk.)
 1. Musicians--Zimbabwe--Interviews. 2. Musicians--Zimbabwe--Biography. 3. Mbira music--Zimbabwe--History and criticism. I. Capp, Kristin, 1964- II. Title.

ML385.C27 2006
780.92'26891--dc22
[B]
                              2006035488

Table of Contents

Introduction

From 1986 to 1994 I traveled and lectured in sub-Saharan Africa. My immersion into the richness of African music instilled a desire to find a way to help preserve this traditional African music. A collection of images, an odyssey: In a café in downtown Harare, Zimbabwe, savoring an African meal of sadza and "relish" while listening to a female Shona musician dressed in a shimmering long white gown and turban; sitting in a huge arena listening to a Zimbabwean band dressed in colorful traditional garb, playing popular and traditional African music while hundreds of people dance; perching on concrete bleachers in a massive outdoor sports stadium with squawking birds flying above and a soccer practice underway on the field, while talking with a poet-musician about his life as a herd boy in South Africa; relaxing in the warm sun in the back garden of a musician after she has stopped by the local hospital to feed her just days old baby, which is still in the hospital; sitting in the tiny lounge of a Shona home in a "high density suburb" being welcomed by young children who are relatives of the musician, singing a special song and dancing. These moments and many more gave life to this research project. In 1999 I returned to Harare, Zimbabwe, to investigate and learn more about Zimbabwean music and musicians.

The starting point for talking about Zimbabwean music and musicians is the mbira, a lamellophone, which is a percussive instrument consisting of a small wooden board or box onto which a number of metal keys have been attached, with metal objects or shells added to produce buzzing. Historically, the mbira was important in Zimbabwe very early, but it was not played as much during the colonial period. There is renewed interest in the mbira in Zimbabwe since Independence from colonial power in 1980, and it has become increasingly popular throughout the Western world in recent years. Most of the musicians interviewed here know the mbira well and have been influenced by it in their music making. I studied the mbira in Seattle, Washington with Dumisani Maraire in the 1980's and in Harare, Zimbabwe with Sam Mujuru in 1994. Thanks to Dumi, Ephat Mujuru and other Zimbabwean musicians, it became common to hear mbira and marimba groups at local festivals around the Western U.S. from the 1970's until the present. Their music was energetic and infectious, audiences loved to dance to it.

While lecturing and performing in piano at the Zimbabwe College of Music, I collaborated with Ephat Mujuru, a Zimbabwean musician, an mbira player, who is included in the collection of interviews that follow. This interview was the point of departure for a subsequent process of meeting and interviewing thirteen Zimbabwean musicians whose stories comprise the content of this book. Among them were several renowned mbira players, popular musicians who have bands of their own, an ethnomusicologist, a jazz guitarist, several leading women musicians, a praise-singer and poet, and a Cambridge trained musician and dancer. I chose them because of their reputations as being excellent musicians, the variety of backgrounds and experiences they represented, and their availability for me to interview them, both in Zimbabwe in 1999 and in Monterey, California in 2001 at the Zimbabwe Music Festival. Some are currently performing, while some are involved in other areas of musical activity.

The interviews took me to the workplaces, homes, and performance venues of the musicians. From the first interview, two themes emerged and permeated many of the conversations. The first was the importance of keeping traditional Zimbabwean music alive. The second was related to improvisation, a kind of spontaneous music making done by musicians in all music cultures. I asked most of the musicians how they think of it and do it. They had different ways of talking about it, but our ways of improvising had much in common.

The musicians' stories were not only fascinating and varied, but also sometimes emotional and thought provoking. These musicians came from all kinds of backgrounds and were dealing with tremendous obstacles—poverty, lack of needed training, lack of marketing skills, no means to pay for marketing, and so on. But there were some wonderful successes—traditional music re-emerged and thrived after Independence, music was brought into the schools in Zimbabwe; regional and international fame was attained by some of the musicians. I became convinced that these stories needed to be told, not only to Zimbabweans, but also to those outside Zimbabwe who have a deep interest in Zimbabwean music and to those who are encountering it for the first time. Because improvisation was the point of departure in the interviews and was a common thread with all the musicians, each interview became an improvisation. The lives and dreams of the musicians are chronicled in the stories that follow.

Myrna Capp

Harare, 2000

OLIVER MTUKUDZI

Oliver is a tall, lean man, soft-spoken and gentle. There is a warmth and a thoughtfulness. He seems to have a balanced view of himself and what he does as a musician. His sense of humor sneaks up on you, takes you by surprise. He wears well. When Oliver came to Seattle to perform at Bumbershoot, we shared a leisurely barbecued salmon meal together in our back "garden." Oliver spotted a blues photography book on our coffee table and before the afternoon was over, was tucking it into his luggage to take back home to Zimbabwe.

My interview with Oliver took place in his home outside Harare where we waited for him to return, and visited with his daughter, Samantha. We were served tea, and had an opportunity to get some insight into how much Samantha cared for her Dad, and loved to spend time with him, especially on tours, meeting famous stars, like Cher and Bonny Raitt! Oliver's home is like a haven away from the bustle of the city, providing a place for him to have an oasis from the hectic life he leads.

As an internationally known performer Oliver is often away from home traveling and missing his family. Fortunately, he loves to perform, so any disadvantages in his performance schedule are outweighed for him by the sheer joy of sharing his music and having audiences respond so positively. He continues to do live shows and produces new CD's regularly.

Oliver's music has a refinement. He has something to say—something important! He wants to do more than merely entertain. He is savvy about what will work musically and what will not. He wants his songs to have staying power with people, although he moves on to new musical ideas for himself. His shows are "tight," maintaining intensity and energy. They present a variety of styles, are visually satisfying. The colorful performance outfits add punch to his shows, and the audience involvement is palpable. People MOVE...dancing, clapping, and singing! Oliver's hit songs are known and loved by many in his audiences as evidenced by their singing along, both in Zimbabwe and in the States.

Oliver calls himself a social commentator, but he is also a cultural ambassador. He is not in the business to make a lot of money, although he happens to be currently the most successful Zimbabwean popular musician. He wants to entertain and quietly educate people about issues such as AIDS. His music, which is very popular in Zimbabwe and in the West, possesses a scintillating mixture of styles, especially rhythms. It is happy, upbeat and well suited for dancing. The instrumentation is a mixture of traditional Zimbabwean and Western instruments, while Oliver's vocals are completely his own, and have been described as big and sensual. As Oliver told me, "The song is what the audience remembers, cares about. Not you, the performer. It's the SONG!" The appeal of Oliver's music reaches into country western music in the U.S. where Oliver is included on several CD's by Bonnie Raitt, popular American rhythm and blues, folk, rock music vocalist.

Oliver does not consider himself to be political, but he does feel cultural/social responsibility to reflect how people in Zimbabwe feel about what is going on in the country. He avoids controversial topics in his lyrics, and instead, uses an indirect approach to addressing problems. Oliver focuses on individuals having self-discipline and taking responsibility for their actions. Oliver has written and staged a musical and starred in films, including the internationally-screened "Jit," a film about Oliver's life and music, which has been shown at various festivals in the Pacific Northwest and elsewhere. The film is an appropriate way to celebrate a musician who is a wonderful representative of his country.

Myrna Capp: When you were talking about your early life, one thing you mentioned was about your parents who were both in choirs—in different choirs. Sometimes they asked you to be the judge.

Oliver Mtukudzi: Yea, and that was how they came to meet. I mean... she was from a choir and he was from a choir, and it was like—at a choir competition. That's how they came to meet and so that competition stayed at home. Mom would sing her own song and Dad would sing his own, and they would compete in the house, you know. And us as kids would be judges as well. Who did it better? That kind of thing.

MC: Okay, you were surrounded by music all the time then, because of that. So then when you were in school, you were singing in choirs, but you didn't like that choir music very much; you wanted to do your own music!

OM: Yea, I used to run away from those school choirs, because I didn't like to be told what to sing—especially to sing a song that has been created by somebody else. I wanted to create my own song. That was the feeling, and I used to run away from choirs, but if it served some function at school, and they asked me to put up an act or something, I would go there and sing my own song.

MC: And you mentioned that you would like to have gotten some help in your music education from the College of Music, but that it was not open for you and you couldn't afford it.

OM: Yea; I mean, we couldn't afford—I mean in general schooling was a problem, getting fees for academic education. We were a family of six. We were too many for one person's income. So it was difficult to go to school. Later on, getting some money to go and learn music was like—nonsense. You can't just even think about it—you won't even think about it. The basic means, income, is not enough.

MC: And then, how you got in to starting music as your career. Can you remind me of how that happened?

OM: Well I don't really know. If I was a person who sat down and thought, what would I want to be in life? Yea, I would like to be a musician. Yes, then I would be able to tell when I got involved in music. But it was something that was in me from a very tender age. I just loved music and I just loved creating my own music. So I carried on and that was it. So I can't really tell when I started.

MC: When you got that guitar, that was an important turning point wasn't it?

OM: Yea it was, or not really a turning point, but it was a step further, an improvement, a development, you know?

MC: We talked about your wanting creative people to work within your group—not necessarily serious musicians, but creative people.

OM: I mean, creative people! You have to be serious, but that's not the important part of the issue here. It's not how serious you are, but how creative you are that works, You see? The group members are very creative people, you know? They're alright as personal musicians, but they're very creative, in the sense that, although I do write most of the songs and arrange them, they also challenge me and come up with something better than what I arranged.

MC: Both with the music, and with the lyrics?

OM: Yea. In most cases just the music. The lyrics, normally they don't even tamper with them.

MC: I was reading in one of the guidebooks for tourists, that the lyrics of one of the most important songs you did early on was about AIDS.

I was wondering what other topics you've written songs about. Talk more about the topics that you choose—political things.

OM: I don't understand the word "politics." Although most people have tried to explain it to me, I still don't understand the word "politics." I've got these feelings that I live in a community, I live with the people, I stay with the people. I wonder if their feelings are politics or what. I just talk about what they feel, what we feel, what we think we should do, and what should be done in this society, what's wrong with our community and such things, you know? If that's politics, then I must be a politician. I don't know what's "politics" anyway.

MC: So you wouldn't probably sit down and write a song about the Constitution dilemma that's going on right now, that wouldn't be something you would do?

OM: No, but I have been involved with a Constitution song. In that song, my message really is, "People get together. Try, and you can start a Constitution! It's for your own good, it's not for the government, it's for us! Go ahead and do something about it. It's up to you to do something that you feel that's going to be the right thing for you. It's not for the government, it's for you, the people! So I'm not really a politician, but I can see it's worth doing it. We have to do it. If you want to have proper guidance of your everyday living, then you have made that guidance.

MC: How do you keep up on the news and current issues? Are you reading the newspaper all the time? Are you watching the news on

TV? Are you speaking with your friends? How do you keep in touch with things? You are so busy.

OM: Well, I do read. I do a little bit of reading, especially if it's musical, then I get a little more interested. But I do read newspapers. Each time I buy a newspaper, the first page is the entertainment page, then I go to the cartoons, then a little bit of sport, and then—hey, what else is in this paper? That's when I browse. You see, I'm that kind of person. I'm the opposite of my wife. My wife is like—she doesn't want to miss the news. And at times, a different channel has got my favorite program, and during the time there's news, we are fighting. She wants the news and I want the program, you know? And she's always updating me with current affairs which is happening around.

MC: About your songs, I like the way you said it before, that you want your lyrics, you want your songs, to have a message—but you really have just now said the same thing in different words, I think. You like the idea of a message.

OM: Yes, I believe in a song that teaches me something, that makes me aware of something, that's sort of educational, that's got meaning to me, that reminds me of where I'm going wrong or where I'm going right. Such songs, you know? I believe in such songs, so I think that has sustained me for all these years.

MC: Somebody said of you that you are a very moral man and that discipline is important to you.

OM: I think that's the umbrella that I use in all my songs. The umbrella is not only discipline, but self-discipline—the way you discipline yourself—the guidance you feel—this is good—this is not good for me. If this is not good for me, I'm sure it's not good for her or for him. If you know those things, if you are self-disciplined, you're likely to be the best individual on earth, because you consider other people too. I mean, you are disciplined.

MC: Did you get some of this from your upbringing, would you say?

OM: Well, that's the teaching of an African culture. I can't say it's from my own family, but that's African. That's us! You have to be self-disciplined. You get to a place—you have to make sure. I have this song that's called "Mwana wamambo," meaning that if you are a king's son, you're only a king's son in your father's territory. If you go to a different territory you're not a king's father, you're just like anybody else. So when you go there, don't put yourself as a king's son, put yourself as an individual, as just an ordinary person, and let the king's son of that territory be the king's son. It takes discipline to do that.

MC: As far as the various musical styles you do, we purchased a couple of the tapes (CD's of Oliver and his band) and I've been doing some listening. I'm really enjoying the different styles I'm hearing on those two tapes—with you and your band, and just you with your guitar. I've heard the description of your voice. Could you make any comments on which you liked better of the various styles? Which you think you do the best? Do you like them all?

OM: Well, let's take song by song. I like every song I make. When I put it out, I'm satisfied that this is okay for the particular time. But as I listen more to it, I feel I missed something. I need to develop it from there, whether I'm on my own or with a band. I'm never satisfied that this is the best I've done. But every song I've done, I just like the song.

MC: That's a good answer. Didn't we talk a little bit about the mixture of the traditional music, with more current music, because a lot of people who write about what you do, say you are hanging on to your roots—the tradition. But you are also bringing in these new things that we mentioned the other night, influences from all over Zimbabwe. I guess you could call it fusion.

OM: Yea, it is to me as fusion, because I'm very experimental, you know? I do experiment with the different types of traditional rhythms of Zimbabwe, like "jiti" the "mbira," "dandanda," "katekwe," "mbhakumbha" and those. It's very characteristic of racial groups, for the different types of rhythms, and I try to fuse that. If I play the song, one who likes jiti must be able to hear elements of jiti in that song. It's sort of difficult to do, but it works at times. It's just there. So my music's sort of fusion of all these things. My fans really learned my music after my name, but I was the last person to know that it's called "tuku" music. Anyway, how I do it—it's a fusion of Zimbabwean music. That's why I'm able to maintain it as one hundred percent Zimbabwean music—because it doesn't got outside influences. It's mostly Zimbabwean music.

MC: You mentioned some of your worst and best experiences, and one of the worst, of course, was that Rusape concert where the acoustics were so awful.

OM: Yea, I didn't forget that! The hall is called Vengere Hall. It's still there. That was 1975, I think. That was my first day to actually perform using an electric guitar—to play in a band in front of the audience. So, I was very confident, you know? "I'll show them what I can do." But I couldn't make it—I mean, the acoustics were so bad! They are still bad until today!! Nothing has been done to that hall, it's still the same old hall.

MC: They need to tear it down, huh?

OM: No, I think it's nicer if they keep it like that because it keeps the awful memory of it alive for me. There was this echo, you know? If you strum the guitar it goes "WOW, WOW, WOW!!" and I didn't know which sound to follow when I sang, you know? So I was always singing at the wrong places, until the audience was like, "Hey, off the stage, off the stage, we don't want that new guy!" and so I got off the stage. The next day we were playing in the same town in the stadium, and there it was okay. So when I went back, the people who were my previous night's audience, they didn't like me at all at first, but when I sang then, they were like, "Wow, this is nice!" That comforted me, but otherwise I'll never forget that!

MC: Then I remember you mentioned the one in Mutare where there was a lot of rain.

Kristin Capp: Wasn't that the first live album in Zimbabwe?

OM: I think that's the only one. I haven't heard of any others in Zimbabwe—live recording. It was in Mutare, 264 kilometers out of Harare. I had to take the studio (crew) there. I pulled the studio to Mutare. The public address system, the front house, everything. And four days earlier I sent this company to go and erect the stage. They did a real good job. And the day before, I had to go there to make sure everything was in place. As I got there, I found that the stage was alright, but all the equipment was there in the corner. And it was pouring rain, like nobody's business! I was worried about where they set the equipment, and how are we gonna cover this equipment? But they never even got the chance to set the equipment. It was like heaping the equipment in the corner, and waiting for the rain to stop, and it never stopped.

As I got there, I looked at my watch, and it was late. We were supposed to have our sound check in the afternoon, and there was no sound check, nothing. It was pouring! And that made me sick, and I was thinking how much I've wasted on the whole program, and there are no refunds on these things, you know? If rain comes, that's it, it's gone, it's finished! So, lucky enough, the rain stopped quite late and these guys just worked like anybody and set up everything. We did our sound check, but it was not the proper sound check, because there was no time. We did our sound check into, like gates opening, and people coming in. I expected a few thousand people, but there came sixteen thousand people to the show, and they opened only two gates, and those two gates were not enough for the whole. And they opened more gates. My mind was on the recording of this live album because I needed the crowd. So that's another experience I will never forget in my career.

MC: (I asked about the value of having a manager, e.g., Debbie Metcalfe)

OM: Before I met Debbie, I had a friend of mine called Jack Sadza, who died in 1985. This guy was sort of a music promoter. He used to put up gigs, get groups, have little festivals, and so on. No group at all believed in a manager at that time. We didn't know if a manager is of any help in a group. After all, we just were making the number of people going in and out of the gate expand. So most groups didn't like the manager idea. I thought, well, let me try this guy. Because I was kind of busy, and I thought, if I could have somebody else who can go there and book a show for me, that's how we started. But it wasn't like getting a manager, it was, I need somebody to book a show for me and do these two things. So I talked to this guy, and he said, "Okay, fine, I can do that; that's my job. You know me. I do book these deals." And I found this thing is working out, because we used to rehearse five days in a week, and during those days there were times I wouldn't turn up for rehearsals because I was trying to go to Gweru to book a show, and coming back. But this guy would go there and do that, and I made it to rehearsal, and wow, it sounded great! It felt nice, you know? And so he started thinking on his own, I think we must do this, and he started implementing his ideas, and to me, it was nice, ideal! He was the manager.

So that was that, until his dying day. So when he died, I had now tasted the use of a manager. Some other groups used to laugh at me, "What do you need this guy for, you can do this on your own." They didn't understand that, yes, I can do it, but it consumes time for something else, you see? So, in '86 I met Debbie, and she was running a recording studio, Front Line Studio. So, as I went there and recorded there, we just talked and '87, '88, I think it was '88, '87, she started having problems with the running of the studio, and she had to do away with the studio. She was just a person that was born

musical. She understands that she never liked doing anything else besides anything that has got to do with music. I didn't even really appoint her to be my manager, but we just got together, and from when she could arrange a show for me, that's it. We are like that until we did this Mutare concert, this live recording. She was involved

and she worked very hard for that and from there she never stopped, until now, I mean.

OM: We have worked very well for the past fifteen years. Very well, no problems at all. And then, of course, in this business you have your hiccups, but we come to an understanding, and we know our fight is to make this thing work, you know? Which is a good thing, you know? Until now, we are okay.

MC: What next musically for you? As I recall, the way you talked was that you would just be happy if you could keep being the creative person that you are, being able to carry out these creative musical ideas that you have.

OM: I think that's what I am, that's what I can do best. I like to experiment and I'll keep on experimenting.

MC: You mentioned that you were at WOMAD in Seattle? Were you also at Bumbershoot?

OM: Yea, I was at the Bumbershoot. In fact, my US tour—started with the WOMAD Festival. I did a weekend in Seattle, and this particular festival is so unique, because a friend of mine could cancel her schedule to accommodate me for the whole weekend, that's Bonnie Raitt. She came to watch me for the whole weekend, and it was like, wow! I'd never met Bonnie Raitt before, although we have been corresponding, so that was our first time to meet and spend the whole weekend together, and from there on we toured the whole country. We did about twenty states, and our last one in the states was Bumbershoot in Seattle again.

MC: Your daughter was mentioning that you had met Cher and Whitney Houston, and I could tell your daughter was quite impressed.

OM: Yes, yes, yes! We go up there and we go to watch. During the tours, we go to Cher's show. We happened to be off that day and wow! We got there and we managed to see her. And Whitney we met in Germany.

MC: I read that you gave Thomas Mapfumo credit for influencing you a lot.

OM: Well, what really happened with Thomas, we played in the same group for awhile, you know? And we were both doing copyright music. I was doing soul music, he was doing sort of pop music, you know? And he started it all. He stopped playing copyright songs, and he was writing Shona songs, and first songs, second songs, and I felt he was doing the right thing, because, in the first place, that's what

I wanted to do. That's what I wanted to do, and I wanted to play in a band, but the band management wouldn't allow me to do my own songs. They wanted me to do the copyright songs because they were popular then, you see? So that's how I came to do the copyrights. But it wasn't long until Thomas started doing his own thing, and I felt he was doing the right thing. I mean, where would this take me to? I would rather sing something in the language that our people here can understand, something that's us. It was a lot easier doing that than doing the copyrights.

MC: It makes a lot of sense. I think that the description of your voice that included soul, which several have suggested—that the quality, or the timbre of your voice is particularly suited to soul, do you agree with that?

OM: Well, what these people write is their opinion. I can't really challenge that, you know? They are a better listener than me, listening to my own voice. They know better, maybe that's it. I just get interested in my voice when I record a new song, and I'm just finding out if it's done right or wrong, you know? As soon as I'm done with one song, I have another new song. It's out. It's nice when a song is new, but it's different when somebody else listens to my voice. They can treasure that song for years and I seem to challenge that particular performance. "No, no, no, I shouldn't have done that like this, I should've done it like this," you know?

MC: Yea, we musicians are doing that all the time aren't we? I've been doing some improvising on the piano, with Ephat Mujuru doing mbira. I listened to the tapes and I criticized myself the same way, "Why did I do it that way?"

OM: "I should've done it this way." And if I do it that way, you still want to change it— you still want to do it better than that. So it goes on and on and on.

MC: Yea, I think Western musicians are always criticizing themselves, but from what you're saying, you're doing the same thing.

OM: Artists are artists. I've worked with Chinese artists. I worked with the Shona, even the East African, the West African. As long as you're an artist, we speak the same language. We may not understand each other, I mean language-wise, but the fact that we are all artists, we've got no problem with each other. We just click like that in concerts. Even in social life, artists have their own way of telling a joke and if you are an artist you understand an artist's joke much faster than anybody else, because, I think we must be the same people. Never mind our races and our colors and so on. As long as we are an artist, we have this common thing that we understand each other. I think that I believe in that.

MC: Were you in New Orleans?

OM: Yea, I was there. We performed in New Orleans at the "House of Blues."

MC: Do you like blues?

OM: Yea, I do. This son of mine, he's playing guitar and he created his own song. I listened to it. It sounds like blues. Wow, this should be blues!

MC: Are spirituals African?

OM: Yea, they are, because what happened—it's a pity we just met and you're leaving. We could go down and visit the rural areas where they do these ceremonies and you could listen to them when they sing their songs. Performance-wise, the spirituals, you can tell, this theme, you must have heard it somewhere.

MC: When I was playing "Swing Low," Ephat said, "What's that? I don't know that." And I played it for him on the piano, and I said, "That's a spiritual—African American." He said, "That's...I hear it...that it's African!" He detected the African roots of it.

MC: Is gospel African?

OM: I don't know what you call gospel. I believe gospel is not a tune, is not a harmony. Gospel, I think, is the lyrics in a song. The lyrics in a style of a song determines whether a song is gospel or not. I don't think it's the style of playing that makes a song gospel.

MC: I visited in Tennessee—Nashville—and I was told I would hear some wonderful gospel there. I went out to the outskirts of the city to a church, and it was quite an experience. I felt like I was back in Africa because of the feeling...that felt African to me.

OM: I mean...gospel is the message. It's what you're talking about that makes whatever you call gospel. A song, or the preacher, or whatever, it's what he's talkin about, makes it gospel.

1999

EPHAT MUJURU

Ephat and I became good friends in 1999, when he invited me to improvise with him, combining Shona mbira and piano. We met on a fairly regular basis, taping our sessions. The more I listened to our taped improvisations, the more I became intrigued by the possibilities. We were both interested in improvisation, but from very different perspectives. Ephat was a talented mbira player, having performed in Zimbabwe, Europe and the U.S., and had produced several CD's. My background was in classical piano, with some experience improvising in various styles, including classical, sacred, and a little jazz. I studied the mbira briefly with Dumisani Maraire and Sam Mujuru.

In October of 2001 Ephat was on his way to a residency at a college in the U.S. when he became ill, after arriving in London. He was rushed by taxi to a London hospital, but unfortunately he died of an embolism on the way. News of Ephat's death was a shock to his friends all over the world. I have vivid memories of being at Ephat's home in a high-density suburb on the outskirts of Harare on a hot December day in 1999. My husband, my daughter and I visited with the family and shared Christmas cookies and cokes. Ephat gave one of his sons some money, sent him out, and he soon returned with some wood for a small fire. We watched as Ephat and his son, Sylvester, woodburned their names on the drum and mbiras which we purchased from them that day.

Ephat had a dream that we would produce a CD of our mbira and piano improvisations. I kept him informed of my progress on editing the tapes through e-mails in 2000 and 2001. Ephat's music making and his personal warmth and enthusiasm were inspiring to me and many others. It is with sadness that I realize that he will not be able to see and hear the fruits of what we did together musically.

Note: Since the above was written, Ephat has been honored by verbal tributes from around the world, and several CD's and tapes of his music have been released in his memory and to benefit his family. Although he was discouraged and did not feel appreciated for his contributions when I interviewed him, it has become clear that Ephat endeared himself to many people around the world, and was valued for who he was, and for his musical contributions far more than he realized in 1999.

Myrna Capp: I want to know a little more about how you got started with music? What was music like in your family, when you were young?

Ephat Mujuru: Yea, you see it is very interesting. The way I started, it was from my grandfather. My family, a long time ago, they were very popular in making musical instruments, and also in making agricultural tools. Yea, and we had an empire called mbira empire. And then the Monomotapa Kingdom included our great, great grandparents. And they were making music there. My grandfather was a very respected person, who was respected by all people from all over Zimbabwe. And they used to have three ceremonies every year. One ceremony to introduce new crops, and another one was after harvesting, and another one was to ask for rain, and also to thank for the rain that we've got. And when I was born, I was born in a village where there was hardly not television, no radio. We didn't know what a radio looks like. We didn't think that the music comes from the radio. We only grew up in a village where we could see people playing their music. Live music. We didn't know that music could be recorded and then you could hear it. Yea.

My grandfather used to play mbira. He was a very good mbira player. Yea, and he taught me how to play. And that's the only music that we have in our village, mbira and drums, and there was nothing else. We had no radio. Everything we had to create ourselves. At night we could also go out and sing, so it was very much the visual, like when it's the moon, like when there's the moon shining. People could go and dance, and they know, reflecting the moon was like, the whole context was like when you see people dancing, it was like the television, seeing people on television, and also people playing the music.

MC: So was your family unusual in that you were doing so much music, or did all the families in the village in that area do the same?

EM: No, our family was very unusual, because it is the time when African music was discouraged, and a lot of families had forgotten mbira. I'm not trying to praise my family or what, but this is the truth that when you go in some of the areas, they kept to the tradition, the mbira tradition. It was like a small fire, like, you know, like they've kept it, no matter how difficult it was. It was during those days, because it was very difficult. Anything that was African was not really allowed/valued. But my family didn't worry, they just kept on and I don't know what made them be what they are. And our grandfather was a very, very *just* person. He was very religious in the way that he, in morals, good things that people valued, he was very kind to people. People used to learn, even some people from different religions would come and would talk to him. And what was surprising was when he talked, he had very much depth, much more deeper knowledge which connected the Christianity and African religion, yes. He was the only person who could really explain it in a much better way. You see the Shona religion itself is not very far away from Christianity.

Communion

Because you know, you talk about the Ten Commandments, all those, everything was there, everything that happened in the Old Testament. So he was very much knowing, a very respectable person,

and he would talk to anybody, anyone with different religions would talk to him. You know sometimes people would talk about religions, you know. The conversation doesn't go very easily so, it was very nice, because we learned to tolerate. It was a very nice thing.

So what happened was, when we were going to school, people were trying to discourage the teachers there very much, trying to be against us. Because it was the time when African music and everything was trying to be discouraged. Everything that was coming from other places, were much better than ours. So it was like a psychological war that was taking place during that time, and my family never, we never, we didn't fight them, you know? We just keep to ourselves, peacefully and then what was surprising was that, at school, my family, they are very bright in the school, academics. The teachers were very surprised. They didn't know. They couldn't imagine a person who plays mbira to be able to be good in academics. Their justification was not, they could not justify as they wanted. They thought somebody who plays mbira should be somebody who doesn't, somebody who plays mbira should not be somebody clever. And this happens, you know, when you know music. Even in other places, people still consider people playing music, they must be lazy, you know? They don't think music is very important. I think you can see that some of the school children, the universities, you know, like the accounting department, some of those very sophisticated people, like computer sorts, they think that they are better than this, so they see somebody choosing music, they think, ah this is not important and they want to cut the aid, they cut the music.

MC: But obviously for your family—and in my family—music is very important!

EM: It's very important! We knew some of these things, so we kept on playing, and then after school I came here, and I started playing mbira very hard. To Harare. I was playing mbira there, then I came here to the Zimbabwe College of Music and started playing with the other people from different places.

MC: How old were you then?

EM: Then I was twelve years, but I was known. People knew me, our place that we played, the different mbira players were coming. It was so interesting. It was after nationalism, you know? Not independence. You see, nationalism, like in the 60's. It's like the first national time, and it was a revival of the music. You would find mbira, you could find mbira everywhere! Everybody—I wish you could see that time because that time the mbira blossomed! It was very, very important! Every place, every place, in every house. We would not play in clubs because the clubs were all run by the system, you know? The government there was suppressing the African music so we didn't play in the clubs. We had our own places. We could play in our houses and in a very simple way, people would play music. Yea, it was all over, became very popular in the villages. Every now and then there was some ceremony, things happening. That was something! From there, I had to make my band and we started playing. We went all over Zimbabwe.

MC: In your band you had drums, hosho?

EM: Hosho and mbira, yea, and then after that we came here to the College of Music. I was not joining the College, I just came to perform here and at that time when we came to perform we were told to sit somewhere. They didn't want us even. We had to use a different toilet. It was very tough. When we played people enjoyed it, but we were told to go on that side over there. That's when I really began to see. When you are growing up innocent, then you suddenly realize something, the world is not right, you see? And then we went to Great Zimbabwe ruins to play there. But when we wanted to buy some food we were told that we should go on the other side, they would not serve us the food. That place is a cultural place and a place of mbira. It made me very unhappy because I didn't know why things could happen. We're not allowed to go certain places and then I went to a school. I was invited to a school. I was only told to play for ten minutes, so I played for ten minutes.

After that I recorded an album which was called "Africa Where is my Home?"

Africa, the place, she was like Africa imagined. It was like in imagination, because from what I grew up hearing, these were the things that I was seeing, and I said "These people are actually telling me something different, that Africa was like this, but this is not what I'm real actual seeing, this is something different. There's no freedom. So I composed this song which they could not play on the radio, and I recorded it the second time. Then in 1980 I recorded that song, and it is now very popular. It's called "Garuswa." *(Note: I wonder what the song was about?)* In 1980 I founded the first National Dance Company, because in the schools the music was discouraged. And then I found that the energy from the 60's was dying. And then we said, what can we do with African music that people do not know? So I formed the first National Dance Company, which we took to Mozam-

bique, and that first National Dance Company started training people to learn dances from all the regions of Zimbabwe, from Manicaland and Bulawayo. So we put them on one stage.

MC: And so you were doing the instrumental part, mbira and hosho and drum, and dancers with you?

EM: Yes, and that national dance company was called after my name (the name of Ephat's group), *Spirit of the People.* It means that people come together. After that African music was introduced in the schools. That was how marimba, this is how it started, in 1980. Yea, we started, when I was teaching mbira at St. Peters School. I was working with the people in marimba, trying to put the mbira music, African music, in the marimba, trying to encourage them. It became very popular, and the music now is not the same, but the way we started, we were the first founders of the music. Then I came here. I brought the idea of incorporating African music at this school (Zimbabwe College of Music), which was focusing on only classical music. Yea, this place was very difficult, because they could not even appreciate jazz.

So how about African music? It was like something that had not been considered, you know? So I came here at this College and I introduced African music, and then they, of course we had people from America, Indiana University here, and then Indiana helped, and the Ethnomusicology program started. But when it started, when everything got "green" (going), now I was out. I just paved the way, of which I'm not working on that way. I'm just a nobody now.

MC: I wouldn't agree with that. I think you're quite respected.

EM: Yes, but you know I must also get some work.

MC: It's hard now, isn't it?

EM: Yea, but I started the whole thing (African music at the Zimbabwe College of Music).

Note: In conversations with several individuals, I found that there are varying opinions on who actually was responsible for starting the Ethnomusicology program at the Zimbabwe College of Music.

MC: I also want to ask you some questions about improvisation. I know you're really interested in that and I'm really interested in how you do it.

EM: When I see improvisation, a song is played. There's some basic things. When I see improvisation, I see it is a river and it starts very small but it gets bigger and bigger and bigger. Yea, then it has got so many tributaries that goes to this. So the same thing with music, when you improvise, there's the basic. What is the basic? I call it the *missing boat*. It's like the root, the idea, the root note. And then from that, some layers come that look like that note, and then it expands and then from that it goes up. Then when it goes up, it's like a tree now, this tree is growing but it has some other trees that are growing in that tree, and then the tree has got branches, and those branches have got so many branches, that the branches got another branch, which has got another branch, and another branch, and there's got so many leaves that from every leaf there comes another leaf, you see? So it goes on and on and on, but the food of all those branches of the tree, they're all coming from one note.

So what happens, when we start a song, we play, but we can go and play all these other high notes, everything, but we still keep that in mind, where we are coming from.

MC: When you're doing your Shona songs, the ones you composed and you do for your concerts and things, how do you start with those? The same way?

EM: Yea, the same way that we're doing. The root idea. If something has got the root idea its good. But there's another way which I call *fusion/confusion*. What I mean by *fusion/confusion* is that you start something, and you don't come back to where you started. You just go on. If you're asking to play the same thing, you don't know it because there is no root idea. I think I saw that in some places. I think I saw a group in South Africa that was doing that. Everyone was ... "*bum, bum, bum*" (he sings) and another comes, "*do tu do*" (sings) and another one comes, you know? And then there was a lot of confusion, and there was a *fusion* but there was also *confusion*.

So there is that art where there's fusion and confusion but there is the other art where you can really identify, you can put a lot of things, a lot of colors, a lot of things, but you still have the identity Yes, it's like when you hear the spirituals, the rhythms and blues they have one specific idea/melody. But they can improvise and go all over and come back. So in Shona we say that there's a proverb which means, no matter how a person can be crazy, the person can be very, very crazy, you know, really "mad," but they can't forget to eat. So that means you can improvise, you can make sounds but you have to come back. Yea, you still guide the basic notes. Which is the first idea, where you started (Ephat gesticulates and moves to make his point). So you come back to that. So that's what I see when I see improvisation.

MC: That's good. I like what you just said. I want to ask you one more question about that. If you could have your dream, your wish, like for the next five years, or in five years, what direction would you go with mbira, with your music? What's your dream for the future for you and for mbira in this country?

EM: Mbira in this country? I would like to see it in every school, it has been my idea. I'm not trying to praise myself, but I'm just saying that you're asking the right person. Because for all the music now to be popular as it is, I'm one of the people who made it so, although, I don't see the contribution attributed to me now. I don't see as though I did something good. What I would like to say, I'm still going to work, no matter. I'm just going to pave the way for those people who come and drive nice cars, and they still walk on my foot. I would like to see the mbira played in every school, and this is my dream. I think that's my idea and I would like to help to make that happen. The mbira music—I was the first person to introduce it to America. Yea, I've done so many things.

MC: I know you have. Where in America did you first introduce it?

EM: At Seattle. Yea, and I was teaching at the University of Washington in the music department, and I used to live in 45th street just near the University.

MC: How long were you there?

EM: Three years.

MC: I know I heard you at Meany Hall one time. It was the first time I'd heard mbira like that. You were just all alone on the stage.

EM: That's right. So that's the time I did so many things. Besides doing all these things, I'm not very happy now. Because things have, like I started this College, and where am I now?

MC: Yea, it's difficult, but you're very respected around the world.

EM: But I have nothing.

MC: You feel that way, but for me, an American, hearing your CD's and talking with you and hearing you play, it's very impressive.

EM: Yea, I've done a lot, but it's like, it's like *your* work, what *you* are doing. How would you feel, like what *you* are doing in here. We started everything *(not sure what he is referring to—maybe improvising with mbira and piano)* then another person comes and grabs the scene, and you and me are kept out of it; this is something, you know?

MC: Partly it's the nature of music as a career, isn't it?

EM: Yea. It's very difficult you know?

MC: And what you must be doing—I know I am—we're just following this inner dream we have.

EM: Yea, it's good. When I became religious, that was one good thing that has really helped me. Because, when my grandfather died, it was during the time of the war. He didn't want people to fight. He was very, very just. So that is something that has made my soul. No matter how difficult, how people look down on me, but it is something when I think more deeper, I get support, you know, because I know that one day I'm going to die. So one day, maybe I suffer, and I am; but one day I'm going to die and leave all these problems.

MC: It comes in your songs, doesn't it?

EM: Yes, just like an improvisation, no matter how people can look down upon me. But one day we're going to be the same. So that's one good thing. And also when my grandfather died, he told me that I should be really just. In a dream. I tried to ignore that for some time, but I finally followed what he said, because I found that there was no other way, because this world is very, very difficult. So I became religious. Yea, that was one good thing. I don't want to talk to a lot of people, but I just feel that it's the right time to tell you. Yea, so this is one thing that is very good which has kept me in a very good way.

JOYCE JENJE MAKWENDA

When I finally met Joyce Jenje Makwenda over lunch at a café in downtown Harare, I found her to be soft-spoken, unassuming, and very passionate about her many projects. The more I talked with her, the more I was impressed with who she was, and all that she had done and was doing—musician, ethnomusicologist, archivist, mother, lecturer (regional and international), author, award-winner and more.

Although she had little formal training she was a walking encyclopedia when it came to Zimbabwe Township music and a multitude of other topics. I viewed the documentary video she produced, "Zimbabwe Township Music: 1930's to 1960's," and was impressed with its vibrancy in tracing the history of African music in the urban areas. She used archival footage and interviews to explore the impact of urbanization on the African population.

Joyce encouraged me to include a variety of Zimbabwean musicians in my book project—a praise-poet, younger and older musicians, men and women, traditional and less traditional musicians. These wise suggestions broadened the scope of the book.

An important focus for Joyce's research and lecturing was to encourage and promote women musicians and she thus encouraged me to include several women musicians. She had a clear rationale for each choice, whereas my choices, up to that point, were based on availability and advice from a variety of people, whose rationales were not entirely clear to me. Joyce possessed the insider knowledge that I critically needed.

Joyce was most generous with her time, although she was very busy. She seemed to have a sense of the importance of having a written record of all of these musicians' lives. I am grateful for her ethnomusicological perspective and sound advice. Joyce seemed genuinely pleased, if a little puzzled, as to why I chose to interview and include her.

Note: Editing done by Joyce Jenje Makwenda in 2003 is in brackets and italics

Myrna Capp: This will be a new experience because, as you know, the other people I've been interviewing are mostly performers.

MC: It occurred to me after our conversation the other day—and then having interviewed these performers—that you had a perspective and insights that would be a useful thing to have along with hearing from these performers. And I was thinking of the questions that I had prepared for them—they probably aren't appropriate, so I'm coming up with some slightly different questions. But I still want to know your background because we talked about that, and how you see your early influences. How they, over time, have gotten you to the place where you are now. Not a performing musician, as far as I know, but more of the scholar, more of the researcher, and that seems to be surprising out here, because people who are in music, that I'm in touch with now, are performers or teach, but usually both...more emphasis on performing. In several respects you are unusual, so I thought, well, this would be interesting to talk and try to find out how a person like you ended up on that side of it. So first, let's just talk about where you were born and what the early influences were in your family and see where that takes us.

JJM: I was born in Mbare as I told you, in the first Township and actually it was not Mbare. It was called Harare. Mbare was called Harare. And this whole city was called Salisbury. I am the third generation in the area. My grandparents are pioneers in Harare, which was Salisbury then. But the reason why my parents came to Harare, it's because my grandparents on my father's side, my paternal grandparents, they came from a place called Chishawasha. You see, Highlands and Borrowdale—are Chishawasha. Highlands and Borrowdale are part of our—the Chishawasha peoples (land) and when the colonialists came, people were pushed from that which is now my land. It was part of Chishawasha and we, our tribe, we were the owners of that Chieftainship or kingdom, I don't know which. So when people were pushed to where Chishawasha mission now is, my grandparents were not happy. They didn't want to be settled elsewhere, so they came into the city. They walked from Chishawasha—my grandmother was telling me the stories—and then they settled in Harare.

At that time it was not easy for a family to settle in Harare because, you see, the laws were such that a man could work in the city but not the family. So the family was supposed to be in the rural area, but my grandparents were very strong. My grandfather said, "I'm going to stay with my wife here." So they stayed in the city. At that time—if you know where Mbare Musika Market is—there were houses meant for single people. The houses were made of old bricks. I think some of them are there, but some were demolished. It was just one kitchen and the passage, to discourage families to come and settle in the city.

Then workers, especially those who were from Malawi and Zambia, they got to stay with their families. They only visited their countries of origin once a year, or after a long time, since it was far, compared to those who were originally from Zimbabwe and could go or visit their rural homes once a week. And people like my grandparents, who had said they were going to stay with their families, in the city—the authorities were forced to build another place which was like, three rooms—a kitchen, a lounge, and a bedroom. And my grandparents—they stayed there. And they moved again, to a two bedroom house which also contained a toilet and shower, so that is where I was born in 1958, 24th March. You know, it's like my grandparents saw the development of this whole Salisbury, which is now Harare.

My father was very musical. He did not sing. You could hardly hear him hum a tune, but he appreciated music very much. He was different from me because I like singing and he appreciates music.

How he came to know most of the bands is that they originated from his home town, Harare (Mbare), and what he would do is be a door boy/man and would not pay anything to watch the groups perform. This is my grandmother telling me. You know grandparents always want to embarrass their children. She was actually surprised that I admired my father for what he did. My grandmother's exact words were "When your father is telling you about Township music, did your father tell you that he really gave me problems by being a door boy/man?" All the musicians—started doing their thing in the '50's—but my father was born in 1931. So he saw all the musicians who started in the '50's—when he was a teenager in the '40's.

So actually, the whole story started in the '70's when I was a teenager. We used to listen to hard-underground rock songs and my father used to say to my brother and me, "Oh, do you really understand what you are listening to?" It was so noisy to my father. Every time when we were about to go to a cinema, and we were putting on those hippie clothes he would say, "Are you dressed up?" and we'd say, "Yea." He would say, "During our days we used to do these." That's when he started everything, like our music—comparing it to his. We used to listen to jazz music in the Township, and he would start telling us all these stories before we'd go. So it was very interesting. And it was not important at that time, because we had our own music that we liked. So I've been very musical myself. *(It is amazing how the brain is like a computer because all those stories were kept in a certain file. Life has its "click buttons," and when that button clicked this file, the rest was history as they say.)*

On my mother's side: My mother comes from Bulawayo and her family—where she was brought up had a farm, and I remember that is the only way we were exposed to rural life. My mother would take us to her parent's farm and every night before we went to sleep we would sing. And they've got very good voices, my mother's family, so we sang a lot. And then, I began my musical career. When I was growing up I had a small group. We would sing, and I was very serious about meeting every Saturday. And when the Roman Catholic Church again started introducing African music—it was only the two of us—a friend of mine and me. We were the youngest people who went to rehearse with the group. That's how I noticed my musical talent and I used to sing, and you know what my father said one day? He said, "Joyce, when you grow up, go and join the Mohotella Queens," a group in South Africa. It was not common for parents to encourage their children to sing. My mother was from the academy. My father is from this artistic family, so my father said, "You can do it." My mother would say, "Go to the College of Music." But when she went to ask for the fees, she could not afford to pay the fees for me. It was $3.00 then. I am talking about 1973-1974. I can see her when she came from the College. She was really down and she said, "I cannot afford to pay the fees for you. It is very high." I sometimes think of this when I am at the College of Music. It is amazing. Now I am a lecturer there and I can learn any instrument that I want!

So unfortunately they couldn't take me to the school because it was very expensive. Those days in the '70's people couldn't afford it. So I think that's my musical background. But then, after that, I had four children. When I was expecting my fourth child, for some reason I just, I made dresses, that's what I used to do. (I started conducting research while I was making dresses, and the research took over.) I have two sewing machines. But then I just stopped. I wanted to preserve township culture, I don't want it to die, especially the music. That's what I mean to preserve—township culture. So I asked my father, and I said, "You know those musicians." So he thought I was crazy and then he said, go and see. But then, before that I had talked to one journalist, William Musarwa—his brother composed a tune in 1948 called "Skokian." Now it has been re-recorded by about forty artists all over the world. Louis Armstrong...Nick Castern.

A lot of musicians have recorded it. Hugh Masekela—a lot of musicians. So I was very interested in that song. So I used to talk to him a lot. He was a family member and I worked for him when I was campaigning for ZAPU. So I talked to him a lot about the music, and then that very week, when I was talking to him, he said some Americans came, because they learned that the song came from here. He was saying, when one starts being interested in a thing, other people would come. So he wrote a story for the Americans. It was in 1989 when I was expecting my baby. So I stopped, when I gave birth, about one and a half years. I just—I couldn't do research, and then I started all over again.

I went to see Matambo, one of the early musicians. He was surprised, because I told him I'm looking for this and this, and he wanted to know what I wanted it for. And I said I just want to collect it, that was my main end to just collect it, as much as I can, just for myself and maybe for my children. But when I went to see Matambo I was so surprised. I said, "Why are people not documenting this?" And it's like a voice also said, "Which people, what about you? So from there, he gave me the name of another musician and it was like—from another musician to another and their stories were so interesting. They no longer talked about just music, it was everything—music, politics,

education. But then I started having problems getting other musicians. Some had died, some were gone away. In 1959 my mother told me to go to the Archives. That was when she was employed as a journalist. She said, "If you're having problems finding these other musicians, go to the Archives," and now the National Archives became a place where, I mean, it was like from 8-4 p.m. I'll be there every day. At the National Archives of Zimbabwe.

I discovered quite a lot of articles and I was so surprised. From 1953, especially when the Daily Newspaper was started, it focused on Africans, because all the other media was always for whites. At that time the government was not very much for black people actually. So this newspaper covered stories in the townships—music, you know? So I got a lot of information, and I started linking some of what they were telling me, like politics, education—I mean the social structure of the townships—and then I realized that music is not just music, it's just everything! So I spent a lot of time in the Archives and then when I went to interview someone in Epworth, I said, how did you used to dance? And he said, "I cannot dance for you, I'm old, but go to the Ministry of Information and see so and so, and they will give you my films." I said, "What, are you telling me...from the 40's?" And they said, "Yes." My next stop was now...every day I would go to the Ministry of Information, because what I saw...I couldn't believe it.

JJM: We had some films, old films. I would watch them at the Ministry of Information, and I was so surprised. What my father used to talk about, how they used to trace, I started seeing it there. The fashions, everything, even the society who used to come dressed, and because I had gotten information from the musicians and things, I thought of a *book*. Then I said, "I think I can make a *film*." But I had never done anything. I had not even done anything, I had not even done journalism schooling and I think that that was also when my mother was pressurizing that issue. And my father would say, "But she can do it." But then I said, "Let me just do it" and I did it. I did a journalism diploma with a correspondence school. I'd leave the Archives, come home and study. But then, I stopped making dresses, so I had to find something to enable me to get money to travel around going to the Archives.

So what I started doing to support my research—because it was not funded—it was not easy even to approach, because I was a housewife. They wouldn't even take me seriously, so I just said, "I don't want to even waste my time." So I said, "I'll fund my research." I don't even know—I was so much in love with it. "So I started making some samosas (savory snacks). I can't believe it, you know. Now I don't think I could redo it, I think it would just kill me. My day would start like this: I would wake up early in the morning, prepare for the children to go to school, then go to the National Archives. Before that I didn't have anyone to help me, and then when I come back I would help them with their homework, and then make the samosas. I had to make them at night and then put them in the freezer so that I can warm them tomorrow morning at 4 a.m. My ex-husband helped me to sell them, and then I would start my journalism. So for two years I think I used to sleep just three hours.

MC: How did you do it?

JJM: I don't even know. This is what I'm saying, that when I look back, and when I started living a *normal* life, I couldn't sleep. I'm a fairly light sleeper, but that was too much. I only slept three hours because there was so much to do, like doing the laundry. I would do it at night and early in the morning I would put it outside, go to the shops, go to the people in the shops, because once I would sell them, I could get cash that day. And then I would use it, and buy flour again and I fell in love with what I was doing. Then what I started doing was—I had a chance. I was invited to Sweden through a certain gentleman, Caleb Dube, at the University of Zimbabwe. By then I had started giving lectures at the University of Zimbabwe. Someone had discovered me actually—that I'm doing this. But when he asked me to come to the University, I said, "What? I can't teach people at the University. I just can't do it." But he said, "You have the information."

So I went to talk to them about Zimbabwe Township music and some were—like, can you please help—that music is our music. And they said, "It's fine, it's your tradition, it's not our traditional music." When I gave my first lecture at the university some students were not happy because they said I was not preserving what they termed "traditional music," and I said to them that this was my traditional music as it was passed on to me by my parents. I am the third generation of the early urban settlers. I am interested in a culture that I can touch." And I said, "It's *my* traditional music because I'm the third generation in the township, and let me tell you what this music was all about. It was a mixture of African and maybe Western, but you must also know that most of the fusion was jazz, and jazz is from Africa. So what are you saying—if you are saying it's not yours, what will be yours? For me, whatever happened in my country is my own. This is what I'm saying. In my township where I grew up, I'm talking about what I know, what I saw, what I heard—what I can touch, and I would like to present and preserve that!

I will not be able to be like my grandparents, who had time to tell us stories, and we might not find time to pass our history to our children. That is why it is important to document it in the right way and in an accessible way. My grandparents couldn't write, but they taught us through all of this, which was good. I would have loved to be like them. I think I'm wrong to say I don't want to be like them. What I'm trying to say is that I would love to preserve the culture because I won't be able to sit down and talk to my children like they did to us. My father was an exception—even my mother—because their age group couldn't sit down with their children and discuss. There was a lot of pressure to work, work, work. But for them to tell us stories like that, I can't do it. I can do it myself maybe, but how many people can tell their children? So I decided to document that properly, so that's what I am doing.

I convinced them, and lucky enough there were also people like Professor Solomon Mutsvairo. Because of this music, I married a South African. Someone was saying I was very good at winding the gramophone the way the first-year students do, yet, you know who was one of the students? It was Albert Nyathi, praise poet, and now we laugh about it. That's when I started knowing Albert.

When I gave a talk at the conference in Sweden, people thought Zimbabwe was part of South Africa. Some people were surprised that I was funding myself. They could not believe it. So this gentleman was at a conference in Sweden and then I went to give a talk. They always thought of Zimbabwe as South Africa. So the music—we played—and they said, "You are funding yourself?" They couldn't believe it. They said, "You go to see the Swedish Development Agents—Norwegian—I mean all the Scandinavian Development Agents, and they were happy to fund the research. Because what I had started doing now, I was giving lectures to embassies. The USA embassy invited me—I gave a lecture, and when I gave a lecture to different embassies, I invited most musicians and they were also answering questions. That's what I did with Norwegian embassies—all the embassies. So they gave me a fund to complete the research, and I completed the research, and they said, "What do you want to do now?" And I said, "I want to write a book, then will I make a film." They said, "Why can't you start with a documentary?" I said I've never ever done it. I don't know what I'll do, and the person, Programme Officer, she said, "Just go and sit down and write a script, and try and see people who can help you to come up with a video."

I didn't even know that I was the producer of that videotape. *I didn't even know*! Then I went to a friend, and I said, "I must prepare a budget," and they helped me prepare a budget. And they said, "You've done everything. What you need is a "committee, *(a committee includes everyone involved in the crew)* an editor and a sound person. That's what you're going to do." And when I was directing I would say that I want that person to be smaller—when you're starting—and then you make the person bigger! I didn't even know the film jargon. But it came out—that's the documentary. So that's how I was doing it, and I think I had a lot of support, because people also had never heard of a housewife who ventured into things like that. I've always been very musical, but I think I was drawn to the deepest end of everything. I didn't even have the slightest idea, but I think it was also the way I felt about the music. So I did the documentary, and then when I did the documentary it was aired on television. They said, "How are you going to launch it?" And I thought I would launch it with the ZBC, (Zimbabwe Broadcasting Company), so they said to give them a pre-copy and launch it there. And they said, we think it's a good idea, because we think your audience is out there. It was on the 26th of December 1992, and the next day ZBC couldn't handle the calls.

They couldn't believe it! Actually I made it for my generation and the older generation, but I was surprised by my daughter who was sixteen then. Her friends came here and they said, Mama, we didn't know there was music like this in the fifties. I was young in the fifties and we knew these things. I was so happy that I proved myself to this generation. Even my children liked it! So from there, it launched me into journalism although, before that time I had started writing articles for newspapers. Especially one of the musicians—who was a journalist—an editor with a newspaper, he asked me to write articles. So I was writing articles, but then this documentary launched me in journalism, I think. I won the Writers Award and it got a special mention at the Southern African Film Festival.

So that's how I started going around...even in southern Africa, giving lectures at Cape Town, University of Witzwaterstrand, Natal University. They actually wanted me to come every year, but sometimes I can't make it. ZBC asked me to do a series on the "Township" series, so that's what I'm doing now until I finish it. And the Ministry of Education and Culture also asked me to do a radio program for what they call social history, to teach children social history through music, and I did a ten-part series for school radio programs. And I just finished the book. I thought I'd finish it by myself but when it goes to the publisher, I think I will be co-writing it. *(I will be publishing the book on my own, and, I found an editor who is working on the book. I will be the author and he will be acknowledged as the editor.)*

There's a gentleman that helped me when I was at University. Actually he is my uncle, Caleb Dube. He is the one who helped me a lot, but he will not be working on the book. I have someone who is working on the book as an editor as I mentioned earlier. He's now in the States. He's done a lot of research in music himself even in the States. He's from here. He just went to study. So I will be cooperating with him.

I think I worked on the project for too long, myself and I've excelled so much. So if it's not going to match what I've already done—and I accept that maybe you can be very good at other disciplines, but I think what I've done is enough for that book. Yes. I think the editor that I have is very good at his work, and he is directing the book and giving me advice on how to rewrite the book. As I have said, he will be credited as the editor. I can even show you, but then I think someone has to check it. So that's what I've done, and I also did research on women musicians from 1930 to today. That's when I interviewed Mai Muchena on video. I've done the interviews. I'm just waiting on editing, and that's how I interviewed Dumisani Maraire. I interviewed their daughter—I interviewed him to support—or to give his views about how he felt. So I have one and a half-hours of interviews with Dumisani too.

He talked a lot about women musicians, about mbira, about himself playing mbira because of his grandmother, and saying there's nothing like women playing mbira. I mean the women have a chance—such has been very interesting in the way that it's different from the Township music, which is social and everything. But it also shows you where women are coming from. So it's very interesting.

MC: Whoever you said it was that advised you to go ahead and do that video even though you weren't sure if you should do that—they certainly were right, weren't they?

JJM: Yea, and she actually accompanied me to this video production and was very nice. *(The representative of Norad accompanied me to the studio. She was very helpful and gave advice.)*

MC: The fact that you're not *doing* music now—it sounds like, for you, that's not a problem. For you, you enjoy music—listening to it, but being involved with the musicians in documenting things and preserving all of that is a passion for you, isn't it?

JJM: It is!

MC: As performing is for Busi Ncube or Chiwoniso Maraire—it's the same kind of thing driving you it seems to me.

JJM: My fear has always been that I look—maybe fifty years from now, that all of this will be gone and I think I'm—I was very musical, as I'm saying, but then, because of the type—the place—that I grew up, maybe I couldn't really do it properly. But then, I'm happy that I've managed to—I'm still in music, documenting, as you can see, and so I've no regrets. Even when I started doing this, my parents said, this is where you belong. They didn't say, "Oh, you are married and you're supposed to look after—they didn't even say that. They just supported me, or they said, this is Joyce. I used to sing a lot, even at church, but I don't regret, because I think maybe I was being initiated into what I'm doing now. Understanding the people means now I understand the documentary side.

MC: It's important that you did this, and that you did have that performance experience.

JJM: My two children sing. My son plays mbira, he performs at conferences and my daughter will sing a song (*Senzeni Na?*) with Albert Nyathi. If you had seen the video, ah, it's brilliant. It was voted the third best video of 1996, 1995.

MC: Is it available?

JJM: You know what has been happening? I've been giving the video to my daughter—and I don't know what she does with the videos. Then I went to ZBC and they said they're going to dub it for me. Before you go—I think it's very good—you'll also see Albert Nyathi. *(He might have a copy.)*

MC: I would love to. I wanted to see him perform so much, because I had a sense after talking with him that—CD's or whatever—it doesn't give you the whole performance at all. That would be great!

JJM: What do they call praise songs in Ndebele? When they hail chiefs or kings? That's what Albert's saying. *(That is his kind/type of music. He is called a Praise Poet.)*

MC: Do you have some dream—some ideas for the next part of your life? Do you envision yourself doing very similar to what you have been doing, because you enjoy it so much, and you feel it's a valuable service, too?

JJM: I don't know. I think music launched me into a lot of things. It launched me into being a music research journalist, and it launched me into teaching/lecturing. I never dreamt of myself as a teacher/lecturer, and now I teach/lecture music at the College of Music, as you know.

I lecture in popular music—and also what I've done at the School of Music. I started teaching, and my disappointment has been that there are not many women musicians. Every time I get a quarter of the class who are women. When I did my research on women's programs, even in music, women performed—there are not men—I said to myself, can I continue to talk about women's problems in music, or write about them, as a journalist? What am *I* doing about it? So what I've done at the College of Music—I decided to start a fund. I'm fundraising, but it's going to be managed at the College of Music to enable women musicians to comprise half of the class—not a quarter of the class all the time. Of course it's something that had support, and I would like to see women—because what I've noticed is that the problems that...musicians in particular, and especially women have is, because they don't have the education. They don't have the know-how of the industry. So I think if more women can be educated, more women musicians can go into the College and understand some of the things. Then I think we can have better quality of women musicians. So that's my wish—if that fund can take off.

MC: Busi was saying that she had taken some classes there and it was very valuable and then she was teaching there briefly, and she just got too busy. But she really believed in it and thought it was important, not just for women, she was speaking of, but for the African musicians who didn't understand the theory behind what they were doing. They were doing everything by ear and they didn't understand anything about music theory.

JJM: Also there's a woman, she's now finished. She was one of the best in the 80's, in the late 80's and the early 90's. She dances, so what she did is what no one else can do.

MC: What was her name?

JJM: Katerina. But if she had been educated, I think she would even have gone to University teaching. What I'm trying to say is that the children just look at it as performing. But they should teach it so that it remains true to whatever the dancing styles, the music styles are. They should try and see that the traditional styles continue. Through colleges, through universities. So I really wish women could go to school. I realize it has to be some education. The problem with artists is that we are not taught what we do. It's in us, but then we must try and have skills to be in a better position to manage that in us. That's what I would like women to do, and so, as I've said, it launched me into teaching. I'll be teaching journalism again next year at the College. I was invited to Sweden to be taught how to teach other journalists. *(I have won four awards in journalism. The latest has been from UNIFEM. I became the overall winner in population and gender writing, which brings them to five.)* The latest one in 1999 was a UNICEF and Women in Media. At first I didn't want to teach at the College, but then I realized that I cannot be selfish with information that I have.

The College of Music has been trying to have me as a fulltime teacher but I can't. I'm caught between music and media. If I'm going to be fulltime anywhere, even at ZBC—they've asked me so many times to be fulltime—whatever they pay me for the hour, I think for now, I'm not a qualified teacher as such. I'm learning as I go.

So I think it's a very good way of getting trained myself and giving my information—what I know—to the students, so I think for now, whatever I'm getting, it's ok. Especially when there's always room for negotiating at the College of Music. And anywhere that I'd work, even at the ZBC—what I'm happy about is, the ZBC doesn't have independent producers that they work with. I think I'm one of the first independent producers, to show them that independent producers can produce good work. They've worked with me and I've helped them to change some of their ways of doing things, when it came to independent producers. But now, if I want a fulltime job anywhere, I'll get it. So I think it's good that whatever I've done I don't regret. And I would like to continue, like maybe do a Masters—on the education side of things—and I would like trying to understand things—be more scholarly.

MC: Yes, I hear what you're saying, but as I said before, in a way it's just something you need on paper, a degree, and it gives you some credibility, but you know all these things. You're far ahead of many academics with credentials by their names.

JJM: Thanks!

va, 2000

BRYAN PAUL

Bryan Paul is an articulate and thoughtful musician, with a probing, curious mind, always thinking about the broader context of his music. He constantly evaluates who he is as a musician and person, and how he, and his music making, fit into the bigger picture. Although he thinks of himself primarily as a performing musician, his insights indicate that he is more than that, he is an expansive, savvy musician, always listening to new ideas and challenging himself to do more.

Although Bryan likes Latin music very much and plays it, he believes that African music is more complex and interesting rhythmically. He says that Africans might do well to focus on each of the elements of their own music which are unique, complex and interesting. Bryan maintains that Africans hear music from the U.S. and Europe more than they hear their own music. The reason, of course, is that there are CD's and tapes of Western music easily available almost everywhere. It is much harder to find CD's and tapes of African music, especially from certain areas, although that is slowly changing. Bryan implies that Africans need to know their own music, and use their own musical ideas, rather than being so heavily influenced by music from the Western world. Bryan observes that it is hard to find music in Africa without Western influences. This is a fact of life for him.

I regret very much that I was not able to go to Binga, a small town on the Zambezi River, and hear the Tonga music which Bryan described and was so excited about. His description of it reminded me of a very special, unusual taped example of "forest dwellers" or Bushman music from Central Africa, which I have heard. Hearing this genre of music live would be a rare experience indeed! All musicians know that live performance is the best!

By the grapevine I heard that Bryan is now living and performing in the U.K. It is my hope that later on he will be able to return to Zimbabwe because he has much to offer his own country musically.

Myrna Capp: What I'd like to start out with is where you're from originally, where you were born and what those early influences were in your life, especially music.

BP: Well I was born here in Harare—1958—October. I think I've always been interested in music because my Dad used to play. My Dad's piano is right there in the room. He used to have his own group, which was like a dance band playing. I don't know what you call dance music, but you call dance music for the people here—it's like the rhythms that people dance to, like bossa novas, waltzes, and some of the commercial songs of their time. So my Dad had his own group and they used to rehearse in—at that time we had a flat, a big flat, almost like a house. This is what I used to hear from his friends. They used to be all over on the instruments, just excited to be involved with what was happening then—the music—just bashing around.

MC: Was he a pianist?

BP: Yes.

MC: Did he play other instruments too?

BP: He played Hawaiian guitar. My grandfather used to play Hawaiian guitar and piano so he learned from him. My grandmother used to play mandolin and it was just a family thing...everyone learns whatever instruments were around, and then my uncle picked up on trumpet—so he used to play trumpet...my Dad—and of course different people that used to play in the group...you know bands being what they are, there's always musicians coming and going. So they had a regular line-up. At that time the important sound was the saxophone. For the dance music, having the saxophone to play all these tunes. So they had to have saxophones and a basic rhythm section. I used to hear all this music...this music being constant. I hadn't taken up any instrument until I got to high school...well, boarding school...

I wasn't even serious. At that time you'd just play along on the box guitars because ...boarding school...the only thing you could have there was the box guitars, acoustic guitars...so everyone used to come with their own acoustic guitar and that's how we all learned. We learned from just playing with each other...learning from each other...sharing ideas, things like that...and just excited to play what we thought was great at that time, which was rock. We used to listen to groups like "Grandfunk Railroad," that was a favorite, Jimmy Hendrix...all that kind of stuff. That's what was happening, and being a guitarist—we all started playing guitar—so everyone was sort of a guitarist as such, and everyone used to learn these things and everyone wanted to play the lead lines like what Jimmy Hendrix played. So that's all we were learning, and then, we had done musical training, which was a part of the school program. But there was for the first two years, Form I, Form 2, which was very basic, just very basic learning to read, play recorder, the old reed recorder. The teacher we had was great. He could play guitar, recorder, organ, almost any instrument, so the plan was, he was trying to push this whole music program a lot further, because he saw the talent, there was a wealth of talent in this school so he was trying to promote that. That was in Kwekwe.

MC: And was that the same kind of thing that was going on in schools all over Zimbabwe, would you say?

BP: Yes. A lot of the high schools had quite serious music programs. I mean music wasn't anything serious, it's just they had it to give the students a break from more books because the concentration was more on the academic side. So they had a bit of art work, different arts going on, you know. But everyone liked music so the one teacher just decided he was going to do music lessons. That's how it all came about. And everyone sort of picked up on having these music lessons at school.

At home my Dad used to play. At that time he had stopped playing with bands and used to just play at home. So he used to come home and just play the "Girl from Ipanema." I mean, I know all these songs more from just listening to him than from actual playing them or learning them. I've only learned them recently. It's true...some of these songs, I say, "I've heard these songs before," and it's because someone like my Dad playing always at home and somehow those things sink into your mind. And then, I would like to have done piano, but guitar was the easiest thing, so because it was an easy instrument to carry around, it was cheap—you could get a guitar for $6! You couldn't get a piano for that price. So piano was difficult to get around. But my Dad had the piano so I used to mess around on the piano. He showed me a few things like Chopsticks, that was it, and the C major scale. That's all I learned from him. I'm surprised that's all I learned from him. He was quite a jazzy pianist.

And he used to work with a lot of different groups here, and so I should have been a pianist really to follow in his footsteps. That's what everyone says, and it's true. I should have been playing piano, but I never got to that because I was playing guitar. And then what happened—from school we went from learning a bit of music. We managed to get the teachers interested in buying some band equipment for the school, and they did. They bought some second-hand equipment. It wasn't great, but for us at that time it was the best thing that ever happened. So we had a drum kit, electric guitars, bass. And then they said, "Guys, do what you want to do. If you want

to get into little groups and create music, do that. It was quite free. So it became quite crazy because every class had one or two groups. So now we had to start dividing the time up for guys to rehearse and practice because they only had one set of instruments. So we had to share and that's how I got onto playing bass because no one wanted to play guitar. I mean, no one wanted to play the bass guitar and everyone wanted to play guitar, so it was like, who wants to play bass—nobody. So I said, "Yea, I'll play bass because anyone learning guitar—you're learning the bass lines at the same time on the guitar.

So I picked out a bass and that's when I started playing and learning. I was learning to get around on the bass from that time, not really taking it seriously, but just doing it. It was more of the fun of wanting to play in a band situation with a drummer and guitarist. We used to have concerts—end of term concerts—concerts we used to put on—quite good—and then from there, coming out of school, I used to go out a lot to listen to other local groups playing. And at that time no one wanted to hear about disco. Disco wasn't a thing that you would even consider going to. We had discos in the city center. No one would go to a disco. It was, let's go to the hall where the band is playing, and that was it. Go listen to the band and go watch the band, learn from the band, learn from the other musicians. It was at that time our community was quite close, so everyone was learning from each other. And you could go from one friend to the next friend. At that time guys used to congregate under a tree outside the local grocery store and play guitars sharing ideas. We used to sit with them, pick up a guitar and play along with guys there and learn from them.

And everyone basically was self-taught. No one had any musical training. Most of the people I knew—everyone was playing by ear—learning from records and sharing with other musicians. Basically no one could afford music lessons, like to go to the College of Music, because in those days no one could do that, and also it was difficult to get in, because at that time it was very white. So black students and that kind of thing ...forget it! They just made it really difficult for you to get in. I tried to get some lessons. I wanted to do piano and I thought at one stage, "This is what I'd like to do"...and I couldn't.

They told me that I needed a piano, and they knew I didn't have a piano. So I said the only thing that I could get was an electric keyboard, and they refused for me to take lessons because they said that would be bad for my technique. And I said, at least I'd have a keyboard to practice with at home, so it was crazy. I had one friend,

Denzel Weale—maybe you could research him. He was one of the—at that time—the most prominent pianists that came out. He was one of the best classical students that came out of here. We're talking about black students.

BP: He's now in Johannesburg. He's working for SABC (South African Broadcasting Company) and is doing very well. It was more that you needed money and you had to have parents that were really forceful about wanting their kids to go and be trained there. At that time...most parents...it wasn't important. My music was considered as fun more than anything else.

MC: Do you think that your parents would think you couldn't make a career, a living, with music? Is that why they didn't take it seriously and give you lessons?

BP: It's difficult, because my Dad was actually schooled in Cape Town and he learned a lot of what he knew from musicians in Cape Town, and he did a bit of music theory and all that, but he didn't take it seriously. It's only when he came back here, and he realized that there was a demand to have entertainment. That's when he started a group with some other musicians and they used to work a lot. They were busy every weekend but they all had jobs—they all had their careers, not in music, that they were pursuing, so the music was extra money and they enjoyed it. That was their main thing. At that time there were a few bands that were trying to do it profession-ally and, I think, not by choice, but that's all they could do. Some of the bands were doing that. But even today it's still difficult. It's not something that everyone thinks of as something to do as a career here, you know?

MC: Are you doing it as a career or do you have other work you do?

BP: Well, basically I'm just doing music only. I teach sometimes pri-vately, but now I've been teaching at Prince Edward School helping with the—they've got a jazz group there. So I've been working with the students there mainly doing—I don't know if you can call it a jazz program. We're just trying to "workshop" the students more than any-thing else. Some of them can play, some can't, so we've got students at all different levels. We just try and combine them and make a little group and get everyone interested in playing and more interested in playing jazz because at the moment they're all interested in just the rap ...all that kind of stuff. That's ok. We tell them that's ok, but they get more into the jazz...there's more music happening there.

MC: Do they start to see that, the more they get into it, do you think?

BP: Not at first...it's only when they actually can form some of the songs. Then they realize this is quite cool and they can't help dig it and they go for it. Also the idea that they can now have this freedom of saying I'll take a solo and try these kinds of things—to improvise—it's fun for them, you know? But it's an important step. I keep telling them that's what's happening in jazz. To them it's like a bit of fun because they feel like they're messing around, but a lot of what they play is good. They don't realize that what they're doing is quite good. But for them it's like "Ah!"...which you don't hear in the rap music because everything is quite locked in—pretty set. So now they're playing this kind of stuff where they can say, "Hey, I can play almost anything and it sounds quite cool. It sounds like I'm doing something big." So that's the feeling they get.

MC: I want to talk more about that whole thing and you, because I'm really interested in improvisation myself. Being a classical pianist and being tightly into that so long, and finally recently getting to do a little bit of jazz, I feel like it's so freeing. It just loosens you up, and then hearing what you and Katrina and Sam were doing. I really enjoyed it. And then the German guys (jazz group from Germany who performed in Harare) and so on.

BP: I think the key factor to improvising is the fact that we've been playing. I'm just speaking from my own point of view. I've never been trained specifically or learned things specifically. It's just that of all the years that I've been playing, I've played with so many different groups. I've been playing with reggae groups, disco groups, club groups, groups doing cabaret, and groups doing all kinds of things. So a lot of the time you're not using any music. Everything is done—you learn it by ear. So when you learn something by ear, you're not really picking out everything exact as much as you try—you try to get it all as correct as possible, you know? But once you start playing a gig, or you're playing with a band, you find from week to week everyone is automatically improvising on the initial things that they learned, so the songs are developing. At the same time, everyone's improvis-ing, and as a band gets more together with each other you find that everyone creates more. So it's a kind of natural development in that sense. You're stretching yourself out all the time. Little do you know that you are improvising, even if it's two extra notes you have impro-vised from the original idea. You know what I'm saying?

MC: You're getting ideas from Katrina (saxophone player) and she's getting them from you.

BP: Or other musicians on the stage, wherever it is. And that kind of thing develops, and then you're always having some sort of jam sessions where guys just come up and say "I want to play a song. Can we jam it?" So you've gotta really come up with something and play it. That's good exercise because you have to think of something, and think of something original, and most of the time you're changing your ideas as you're going. So you're improvising constantly. For me that's how I think the whole idea of playing that kind of style has come about.

I haven't learned it from books or anything. I was always into jazz—I've always been listening to jazz. I think that's the most crucial thing. You've got to listen to jazz. You've gotta listen twenty-four hours to jazz, you know? The music's gotta wind in your head, the notes, the vibes, the interaction of what's happening on those tapes and CD's, you know? You've gotta listen to that stuff.

MC: And do you sing it too? Is singing a part of it for you?

BP: I try to. I can't sing. I wish I could sing. I can mess around on some of the notes and things like that, but I wish I could sing.

MC: So you sing with your bass?

BP: Exactly. Yea that's what you try to do. What you hear in your mind you try and play it out. So it's good if you can sing because—I admire a lot of the other musicians, because I think if you can sing, you have a stronger command on what you're trying to do. I know a lot of guys that are very good singers—they've got a good ear, and you find if you say play this instrument, even if they can't play the instrument, if you give them an instrument, they'll play something. Even if they've never touched it, they'll be able to play something because they can hear that sound and they'll find it on that instrument. They can hear it and they'll find it somehow, whatever it is. I think it's important...a crucial thing, you know, if you've got that ear and got that voice. Because your voice will tell you...this is where it is, this is what it is.

MC: The head of jazz piano, at the big university where I come from in Seattle, the University of Washington, his name is Marc Seales (African American), and he is a really fine jazz pianist. I was talking to him as a classical pianist...that I was really interested in improvisation, and he said "Sing!" He said, "You gotta sing...always sing.

Anything I'm doing I'm always singing it first, then I get it onto the piano."

BP: I think a lot of ideas come about—you hear something in your mind and if I think of a bass line, if a bass line comes, it's something that's growing in my mind, and then it sort of gets louder. It starts soft. It gets louder and louder in my mind, and I say to myself, "Damn this"...and I'll go get my instrument and try to find this thing, that I'm hearing, you know? I think the fact that, if you've got a voice, that's the best instrument you have, for anybody. And I get jealous of singers. I wish I could sing the way some of the singers sing.

I just know a lot of musicians that their singing actually makes them play better. That's the way I look at it. And you find those musicians hardly practice, man, they don't practice! I have to work hard at what I play. I work hard, you don't know how hard I have to practice. These other musicians just pick up because it's there, their ear's are there, their voice is there—they find it.

MC: But when I watched you on stage and you were improvising you weren't having to work very hard at it. It's like it just came.

BP: That's because it's been years, man. Years of slugging at this trying to play something. I mean it's only like recently that I'm getting to a point where I can. I'm getting more command of what I'm trying to do, as opposed to sort of playing. I mean you can play anything, but if you want to say something in a certain way that's what is more difficult. Like if you just want to play this certain thing, as the song is going. Sometimes I think, this is what I want to do. Do you know what I mean? If I get my chance to do it, this is exactly what I want to do, that's what I'm saying. A more focused idea, whereas before it would be, you could play something and you'd say to yourself, or somebody might say "Hey that was cool" and you might think, that wasn't what I really wanted.

There's a difference. It takes a long while before you can get to that point where you can say, "This is what I really want to do there." Some other guys just look at me in the band and say, "Ok" even if they didn't like it. I say this is what I wanted to do. It's true, everyone has their turn, you know? I don't know what he wants to do with his thing. And he takes his solo or whatever, so—yea, let him do his thing—see what he wants to say—I think that's what it's all about.

MC: I do too, and that's the fun of it too, isn't it? Now when you practice, do you do scales a hundred times each or what do you do? All keys?

BP: Yea, this is coming back. I'd been playing for quite awhile with different groups and I didn't even know what scales I was playing, didn't even know the chords. I just about knew this was A on the bass, this was G. I knew the notes—and what turned my head around was when we were in Botswana I saw this group playing in the Holiday Inn. They played all this cabaret and they backed up some cabaret singers and then they decided, now they're going to play some jazz, and they started pumping this stuff by Chick Corea and I said, "Yes this is wonderful." And then I spoke to these guys, that's when I found out. "How do you guys get around all this?" I was keen about reading music and all that, but I never really followed it up because I was just playing everything by ear. And I said, "You know you feel like you're limited. There's just something you want to do more, but you can't because you're limited."

Just the knowledge, and all that. You're limited. Your ear can take you so far, but you get to a point where you just hit a wall and you say "No, there's something else that has to be done." And when I spoke to these guys, these guys would tell me, straight after the show at 2:00 a.m. in the morning these guys were going in to practice scales—music books. And I said, "You guys have gotta have a drink, man," and the guys were packing their books and saying, "No we have to practice, it's the only time we can practice between two and three in the morning." Then they sleep and they're back on the job, you know what I mean? Yea, they were getting their practice time between two and five in the morning, and then they would go sleep it off and they're up again.

I saw how serious and dedicated these guys were. And they were showing me. I've got this book, this is what I'm learning—guitar. The drummer has got his music book, so I thought, this is what has to happen. And I came back here and started looking for every sort of basic book I could find, which wasn't much. The music shops didn't have much, so I ended up getting some books on double bass. There's a few electric bass books, very basic, which show you how to read the notation, and bass lines. You go through a book like that and you decide, I learned a few things. Now I know what a minor scale is, and what the fingering is. Now I said, "Just play those things, and then you've got to take it further." I had this book by Ray Brown for double bass, and I said to myself, hey, this is serious, man—all these fingering charts and all this stuff. So I worked on it. I was using the double bass book more than anything else because I had a fat book, like this, and I said, "I've got to finish this book somehow." In the book you go through all the scales—one octave scales, two octave scales, all the keys. You're doing arpeggios, you're doing major arpeggios, minor arpeggios, all the different scales, augmented, diminished scales and all that. I did all that.

And I said, ok, now, so what? I could play all these scales and practice them but couldn't make use of them because I was playing with commercial groups, pop bands, where you're just playing a bass line and that's it. But I knew now what I was playing. I understood more of what I was doing. I could pick out, yea, this is part of an A minor arpeggio or scale or whatever, and then I found I could do more now. I was getting into this idea now. Once everyone was comfortable, the band is sitting ok, I start changing the bass line a little, adding a few other notes, because I knew exactly what I could do with it now. And I knew I was more confident because I knew the notes were right and I knew the scales and the chords. I was getting into that more.

All along I'd always been listening to jazz, so it was something that I used to say, "I want to play jazz." I used to go listen to the jazz groups that were playing here, like late Jethro Shasha, Shona Marumahoka, Chris Chabuka. All these guys that used to play at Oasis motel and you know, you go sit and listen and want to play, and the guys wouldn't even give you a chance to play. You say, "Can I play a tune?" And they would say, "No, you don't know what we're playing"...that's what the reaction would be.

So I went and sat with one bass player. We used to play a lot of jazz. So I asked him, "How do you play—because, from the Ray Brown book I was looking at—12 bar blues and things like that. I said, "How do you play a 12 bar blues?" So he showed me a few things; walking bass lines and how to get round the chords. And he wrote the chord structure for me and said, "These are the chords; you follow the chords, and take it from there." In Ray Brown's book it just had these lines and it made no sense but I could hear the changing to different chords. Now I had the chords so this was all starting to take shape. Twelve bar blues, I used to work on that. I went to the band and I said "Can I jam a blues with you guys?" They said, "Oh no, you don't know what's happening." Until one day these guys called me just by chance. They were stuck for a bass player and they said to come and play. I said, "What do I do, what do you guys want to do?" They said, "Ok, come for rehearsal," so I came for rehearsal and they started pulling out all these charts—"Stella by Starlight," "Night in Tunisia," things I've never heard of.

The jazziest song I knew at that time was...(laughs). It was the jazziest thing I knew, and maybe "Take Five." So they gave me all the charts, and the sax player, Rick, says, "Ok, let's just try it." He says, "This is a swing; just walk the bass, follow these chords." That's what I did. After eight bars he said, "Ok, next song."

He took me through about thirty pages, just the first eight bars. And I said, "No, I can't play this," and he says, "No, we're playing tonight—you have to play tonight." Ah, it was horrendous! So we went and played this gig and it was pressure for me, man! I had to look at all these chords and it was strange, but after awhile it started to make sense and these guys said, "Look, man, we've got all these shows, just come and play with us. So they felt kind of comfortable with me. I was struggling but they were happy to have a bass player that was like following the chords at least, because they were complaining, "Man, these other bass players, they couldn't follow the chords; they're playing the wrong notes—everything. So they were happy—at least someone was playing the right backing for them.

So we just carried on doing these gigs. Just playing the gigs over and over, and I got to know the tunes, the songs. Then I quickly had done this jazz course. And I tell them—and one of the guys was saying I should go do the jazz course. But I said "I don't have the money, and I don't have the time. And then he says, "No, you should do *this*," and I said, "Like what we are doing here?" And he says, "Yea, you're right, this is like a jazz course." And I said, "Look, you've done the course; you just tell us what we need to do, what you want from us, and you can show us things, playing in the band—that's always worked—everyone sharing and showing people different things.

He was great with that, because he was teaching, and he was into that. So every rehearsal was like a lesson, more than anything else. We'd rehearse a song and it would be a lesson. We'd take the chords apart and use this scale and improvise on this, and that's how we used to rehearse. During the gigs that was also important, because at the gig you'd get a chance to try these things, you know?

I started taking the charts home and looking at them very seriously, looking at every chord; looking at the melodies and looking at what scales would fit with chord progressions so that you could improvise and things like that. And at first it was just mind boggling for me. How I think of it now, I think I break it all down into really simple things, like I try and look for more simple scales that fit across a bunch of chords as opposed to trying to play every chord, which is—some guys can do that. It's difficult.

That's what Charlie Parker and them were doing ...they were beating up every chord with scales and riffs and everything. That's difficult. To do it all the time is hard, man—demanding. So it's nice to be able to get to a comfortable way of playing, where you can relax and just say, "I can use this scale for eight bars and make more sense with that."

MC: What do you foresee, what do you want out of what you're doing in the next two, three years? Do you see yourself keeping on doing more of that, when you project ahead a bit? Where do you want your music to go?

BP: You know, I listen. I've got a lot of different music. A lot of it—I get all these different things that come out of New York. These guys like Steve Coleman, and that's what they're doing. They're just pushing ahead. All these different rhythms and different chords and scales and more kind of "out" kind of playing—scales that guys are not really using, like diminished scales, augmented scales and substitute scales and things like that, which is great. But you know what happens—where we're playing here, in this situation in Zimbabwe, people don't understand that.

So you see, when you get groups like the German group and they are playing all these kind of "out" ideas, it's too deep for the ordinary listeners here. People still like to hear the melodies, and the improvised—the melody must be running through it. You can't do something totally weird at all, out of the key center or anything like that, so it restricts the guys from progressing here and going to that. When we were playing with Rick—Rick was a very advanced player—he was playing all that kind of stuff here and people used to look at him and think he was crazy. Like what's wrong with your sax player; can't he play in tune? The people were saying, "We love the band, we love what you guys play, but your sax player, Rick, is doing all these weird things, and then he started toning down because he realized people don't hear what he's doing. He toned down and started playing very cool stuff—this cool jazz and people used to say, "Ah, you've got a good sax player." I used to say to Rick, "These people only hear what they want to hear, they're not trying to hear what you hear or what you're trying to put across. So it's difficult to say, "Can we push further than where we are now?—you can't. The audiences here are not moving with the music like they are overseas. If you go overseas the audiences move with what's happening musically.

In '90 we did a tour with the same group I'm talking about. It was in '90 and we were all over Europe and that's when we felt the difference and we actually felt like we weren't playing enough because of coming from Zimbabwe. We actually toned down all the music, all the ideas that we had originally started out with—we had South African songs and things like that. It was kind of crazy, but that was the kind of stuff they were hoping to hear. We did a few things like that and that's when we realized some of these audiences here understand what we're trying to say. And of course we had audiences that would still come back to—"Play some nice simple African music, so we'd play some of that." We would say, there you go, and what else do you want? So we were quite versatile actually, because we could play a lot of traditional music from here. We were calling it "Afro-fusion," and we would get into more serious jazz.

We were quite versatile—we could cut across genres—which was helping us. Also we could play a lot of commercial music. The one club where we played—there were people asking for—can you play Miriam Makeba or Letam Bula? We had this singer and we just said, "Dori, sing!" We play it and then they were happy. So you see, it's the audiences also that restrict musicians from going further out into

what they want to do. So that's what's happening here. We were trying to take some African music from here and do it with a more jazzy feel. And trying to use some of the rhythms from here as a foundation for that.

MC: It sounds like you could be comfortable just staying here because you understand what's going on, you know what the audiences want, and you can find some satisfaction yourself, pushing ahead as you were just saying, so it works for you here.

BP: Sometimes. I don't know if the audiences know what they want themselves. But they want some of the tunes we write. Some of them do go well with the audiences, they enjoy it, so that gives you an idea, this is where they are. And then you try another tune and you say, ah, this is a bit over their heads, so then you just say, leave that—you use it for some other show. Like when we did this German show, we tried to—I mean most of those songs I had written, and so we threw in a few new ones which—well not new, they're old—but we hadn't played them. But it was good to play them because some of them just don't mean anything to the people listening. So I said to Katrina, let's try these and see how they go. But we still kept it within a sort of reachable sound for everyone.

MC: It seemed that the audience really understood what you were doing. They obviously liked what the German people were doing—it was something different and novel and new, but they related more to what you were doing, in a different way—more.

BP: That's because, it comes back to what people understand, and most people understand grooves. They want to know where the beat is. If they don't hear the beat they don't understand the song. And you see, with the German trio there's no drum so that everything just is floating. You can't even tell where they are basically, unless you're really sitting and listening very closely. They've eliminated that idea. You take the beat away and all of a sudden everything else opens up and it sounds strange. But now for the listener it makes it difficult. But also what I've been trained to do is—because I'm trying to write this kind of Afro-fusion style—you need the drums, because drums are a part of African music. It's a crucial part, and those are the rhythms you are trying to work with and latch onto, and trying to do something with them. So you have to have the drumbeat going, or the percussion or something like that. I don't mind, I can play without drum, I don't mind that. We used to do that all the time, but it just makes more sense to people when the drum is there. If you've got a good drummer, everything just works, no matter what we play.

MC: One other question. I'm not sure how to ask this. What do you think makes a difference for you because you're colored? Do you bring something different to your music?

BP: I think that question has to do a lot with where everyone grows up. When I was growing up, Arcadia was basically the only suburb area where colored people could stay. Mbari—that's where all the black people were staying. The rest was basically for the white people—the rest of the country. So, this is why I said, in those days the communities were more tight, closer, and what used to happen—down the street, everyone knew. So if someone learned a new chord, everyone would know it, you know? And that would happen with the music. At the same time, what we used to listen to—we used to listen to a lot of soul music. It was the main music we used to listen to. But because we were surrounded by white people—black people, you hear what the black music is about.

Grayson Capp: What was the colored section?

BP: Arcadia—this is Hillside now. Then you've got Braeside and Arcadia and what happened was, from Arcadia—just because of expansion the white people moved out of Braeside, Hillside, and more colored people moved toward Braeside, taking up those areas. So that affected how we played, because white music was white music, black music was black, and colored music, basically—I can't say we have a music as such—but we listen to everything. A white song that we liked, it was good rock and roll, or whatever it was, we'd listen to it, dance to it, and play it. So if there was a good African tune that everyone loved like Toko, or Pata, Pata and things like that. We'd learn them and play them. We'd be getting ideas of what was happening with white music, black music, and traditional music.

Everyone used to listen to more of the American soul music. That's where we all get this funkiness in us—this style of playing—musical ideas. So for me, this music that I'm doing is a fusion, it's a fusion of all these things. Like I said, when I started learning guitar I was listening to Jimmy Hendrix, Deep Purple, all the rock groups you can name that were prominent in those days. That's what I used to listen to, so it's a fusion of rock, underground, traditional music, soul music, R&B, funk—whatever—it's all wrapped in.

MC: And you created something special on your own.

BP: Exactly; and then that's how you get your own feel. I can't play bass the way those guys play bass in Mbare. It's hard, man. Those guys they've got their own thing they're doing. I can learn some of it, but to really do it the way they do it, I'd have to live with them for years. You see that makes the difference. They grow up playing that from day one. They understand it, they know it, they do it, and they learn other songs—they can learn—it's the same difficulty they would have trying to play a rock and roll tune as good as a white group would do here in Zimbabwe. It's the same thing. And it works like that. But what I've tried to do, I've tried to be sort of an all around player as much as possible, trying to play as much different music as possible. Like even the Latin music—I love the Latin music, so that's another thing I like, because of all those rhythms and percussion and all that.

It can be *heavy*. But when you're coming from trying to play African music from here—the local stuff—and you get involved in that, and you try and play it after working on that, you find other things actually sound a bit easier. I can relate to what's happening with other music. Other music's easier because some of those rhythms—there's some serious stuff that's happening there which has never been touched. You just hear...like Thomas Mapfumo, Oliver Mtukudzi play ...that's all basic. Not basic, but that's mainstream traditional music. There's stuff in Msvingo, there's stuff in Manicaland that—there's things we haven't heard yet—haven't even been recorded yet! So you only find this out when you play with different musicians from those areas. They'll come in and say, hey, this is how we play and you hear what he's playing. He's playing a different tempo, different feel.

So there's a lot happening in this country. They're only exposing a certain style—traditional music, which is very unfair. You hear the Tongas—what they play! Have you heard the Tongan music? It makes you wonder. I mean those guys play the horns, the antelope horns. There's about fifteen in a group. These guys blow one or two notes on their horn, but when they get together as a combined orchestra it sounds like a complicated piece of music—it is! Everyone has got a different rhythm, everyone has got a different note and the percussion is happening, the shakers are going, the women play the drums and the shakers, the men play the horns. I tell you, by the time they finish playing this tune you don't even know what the hell is happening, because you just stare—mind-boggled with all this rhythm and sound!

MC: You know what you're reminding me of is an example I heard in a World Music class, of Pygmy Bushmen singing, where all these different parts were going; some instrumental and vocal, and there was no particular beat, but it all just *clicked* together (hocketing).

BP: Exactly. That's the Tongan music, and the way they're improvising on the horns to me is what Coltrane was doing on his horn. Only Coltrane was trying to do it by himself, but these guys do it as a group of fifteen. The limitation is because they've got—each guy has got a little horn so he can only get one or two notes any way he pitches it. It sounds like a saxophone. He's got the whole range of notes and scales, but when they're all blowing, that's what it sounds to me like—Coltrane playing. This is what these guys have been doing. It's the traditional thing here. They just do it. Oh, you just see them—you have to see them!

They were sponsored by the Austrian government. They were promoting and trying to help them with their music. They've taken them overseas. They've done a few projects with them to try and help them, because the Tongan people have been left out. They were displaced from Lake Kariba, because they used to live on the Zambezi River. When they made the dam, they were totally displaced, so they are in an area where their food supply is very low; they can't grow anything and they're suffering. And they've got this wealth of traditional music that no one seems to care about.

People are helping them. I don't think I have those resources, but the Austrian government has done something, so that's good. But what I'm saying is, exposure of that music on a local scene hasn't even been touched yet. There's a whole style of music that hasn't even been tapped yet and then some of the Western musicians that came out, when they heard this stuff, they said this is *jazz* they've heard, because that's what it is. They're improvising. The key man starts with one little riff and from there it just goes on and on, and when they perform they do not stand in one spot. They move around, and as they're moving around they improvise.

Wherever they go that's how they perform. They perform on the move—they do not perform in one spot. You can't do that—you can't (laughs). They'll die if they do that. It's so great, man, because it's like music on the move, you know what I mean? Meanwhile while we are standing on a stage and getting all serious on a stage in one spot—they're having fun moving around, jumping around. They go up the hill, they come down the hill. They performed in the park sometime back. They were all over the park. They took their music all over—they take the music to the people. They go here—they don't wait for nobody. That's because that's how they do it in the village. There's a whole lot of—it's quite an old story—there's a lot of reasons

for it but the point being, I think, that's the most improvised music in Zimbabwe—that's what I feel. Mbira music has a lot of improvising that they do, but Tonga music is more serious in its rhythm and improvisation.

I tried to blow a horn and I couldn't blow one of those horns. I don't know how they blow those things. And somehow they're all in tune. And they've all got different horns. Everyone's got a different piece of horn. They've got all kinds—anything that they can make a horn out of, they do it. It's true, but it's so great, and everyone has got his horn. He keeps it, that's his and they go—they train well, the musicians that want to perform. They train for years. It's not a young group. It's all old people playing the music because they feel that the younger musicians—it takes a long time for them to play what they're playing. It's like they've got to go through years and years of training before they're accepted into the group. You find in the group it's all old people, old timers—gray—playing—blowing these horns.

And the thing is—why it's so interesting is that they've been locked off from the rest of the world. It's not like they heard Charlie Parker or Coltrane or anything like that, or what improvising is about, or jazz or pop music. They don't hear that. They don't even have radios, they don't even have electricity. So you know, it makes you wonder. They've developed a style of music that is advanced. It's an avant-style, it's serious. The vibes player from the German jazz group which visited the Zimbabwe College of Music, he was asking me about what music is happening, and I told him about this Tongan music. He was so disappointed he didn't have a chance to go out there. He wanted to go out there and listen to them. But what I managed to do was get a CD. They've recorded some of the playing on CD. Penny Yon has CD's which were done by Tonga people (there is a website promoting the Tongan music; www.kubatana.net.)

Listening to the CD's would give you an idea of where their music lies. It's so much ahead of mbira music. Mbira music is nice, it's fine, but Tonga music is way ahead of that. It's more complex. So you see this is what I'm saying—what I'm trying to do musically is—I'm trying to grab a bit of these flavors with what I know and what I've learned over the years—all the different ideas—trying to come up with something that is—I don't know if I can say it—true to the country, just something different. I've written songs that I haven't even played yet. They're just sitting there. There's a whole lot of songs I haven't even touched. Our problem is trying to record them. You see, Katrina was fortunate; she had the money to go and record in South Africa. She recorded some of her songs, which was great. There's a lot of musicians here that got material they want to record. They can't, they can't record. It's the finances. So in a way, all that is going to waste in a way.

MC: Would you say that for yourself, that is holding you back at this point, the fact that the costs of doing it and marketing it are great? I was talking to one of the head guys over at Gramma records, and he was saying that marketing is one of the biggest problems out here. That's where they need money so badly.

BP: Uh-huh. Well, first of all it's got to be recorded properly. Studios have different prices but you could be looking at about a thousand Zimbabwe dollars an hour. Sometimes you can do a song in an hour. Sometimes it takes three hours. It just depends on the performance and what's involved. So every song has a different time scale before it's finished. This is a limitation for all the musicians. It's the same overseas. It's just that here it's very serious because there's no proper infrastructure musically here—there's nothing really. Everyone's just doing their own thing. The record company is on one side. The studio is one side, the union is one side, the musicians are on another side.

MC: And the recording studios—the message I got was "We want you guys to give us things that people want—what everybody likes, that's what people will buy."

BP: Back to that story—gotta play what people like, you see? Look at Simon Chimbetu and Chopa, all these guys. What they are playing is not really true traditional music. It's a fusion of the qwasa qwasa and the Zairian rumba. They're mixing it with the Zimbabwean music because all of a sudden the Zimbabweans have decided they love rumba and qwasa qwasa. So now the musicians have to record that, or record music that has that feel and similar, which is sad, because they're dumping their own traditional music. That's why I tell people—qwasa qwasa—why don't you guys learn Zairian or something.

One of the biggest things is that we are exposed musically to the rest of the world more than to our own music. So we get more American music than we get local music, and you can hear it on the radio—Radio 3. All you hear is American music. So that's where we get all these ideas from, see. When we get American jazz CD's and records, that's all we hear, those kind of things.

MC: I think it's good that you're giving me all of this information and I hope that between Kristin and myself we can get it out there so people can hear and know a little more about what's behind what you're doing.

BP: But our influences come mainly from your side; that's the biggest influence. So we're always trying to do what you people do, do you know what I'm saying? More than trying to do what we do here, which is different, you see. This is also what we're trying to establish, this link between the sociology of where jazz has come about, the roots. So if you listen, that's why you listen to the best example—it is the Tonga group, because they've been improvising without anybody telling them to do that, and they haven't been influenced by any outsiders. So they are a good control group to look at and say, how did they get about this, you know what I'm saying? We've been influenced, so I can't say what I'm doing is truly myself. But the Tonga people—it's genuine to them, truly genuine to them. I'm sure there's a lot of groups if you're looking around Africa...you can find some things.

You see, this is where the foundation of this whole jazz thing has come about, because African people have this natural idea of just playing. They're not locked into getting technical about—what's this note and learning scales. They just make a sound and whatever sound they make, this is how it goes, and they combine these things just from a natural way. You see, this is why Katrina has been playing jazz with us, and she's had that problem, because she's been classically trained. Now she's trying to play this jazz—play African music. I said "You've been too groomed...you've been over-groomed actually." So now when you want to break those chains, it's difficult.

It's difficult and she has a hard time. She's improvising and always complains—I can't get this, I can't. I say it's because you've got all these chains that are wrapped around you. You've got to get a *cutting torch* somewhere along the line, and free yourself somehow. I don't know what it's going to take, but I can feel the difference, and see. There's a player like Richie, who hasn't been trained. He plays alto, and Richie just has this natural flair, going across the beat, playing notes. I don't even know where he finds them actually, he just plays. Even he doesn't know. I say, "What did you play?" He says, "I can't remember...it's just blue, I don't even know." So you see, it's different. Whereas Katrina—everything she's playing, it's like, technically it's being calculated in her mind, the beat, the note, everything, am I right?

MC: Absolutely.

BP: So you see, too much thought is happening there—too much thought. Whereas it should be just relaxing and saying, "Even if I hit that wrong note I'm going to find another way around it." Overthinking. This is why it's great that, I was trying to say to you, that what I'm doing is try to simplify everything, because if I think of every—if I'm given a chord chart and I think of every chord that I try to play and I improvise on that chord, you end up with a scrambled brain. But if I have a quick look at the chords before that and I can say ok, this is basically what's happening, and this is a scale, a blanket scale—it fits over—then I can have more time to think about what I want to say, because I've got this scale that I know. I can choose the notes, then I can follow and relate some of the chords, and also not to relate some of those chords. So, straightaway your mind is more free and more open to look at other things and look at ideas and whatever.

But of course to get that facility everyone needs to have a certain amount of technique and ability. Of course, you've gotta learn your scales and that's what happens. You find—I don't know if you feel the same way—you find you learn all that stuff, but at the same time you've gotta practice twenty times more to keep it up. Which is a problem. How can you do that? You can't do that, because everything that you learn, if you try and keep that up, you can't. It's impossible. So I'm just basically trying to simplify everything. I know a lot but at the same time I'm just editing all that info and saying, "I don't need that." Because I know I don't need that, so I don't look at it. I need this, I need that—this works, that one works, that one doesn't work and so just leave it. But it's good to know it, there'll be a time when that might come in handy. The one that you didn't use today or that scale that you didn't use today might be the one you use tomorrow.

MC: And if it's in your ear it will come out when you need it.

BP: And in your mind, and in your head, and also if you've got it under your fingers, then that's fine. You can always come back to it. Even when I practice—like you asked me, what do I practice? I've come back to practicing scales. I practice this scale a few times, and I say that's cool, I still remember that. I play A minor scale, or A melodic minor scale and I say, "I'll do it a few times." It's more like a revision, and what I look at is trying to break up those scales and see what kind of pattern is that. I spend days just trying to make up patterns out of those scales. They're in the books. I've got some books but sometimes you don't have the time to say, " I'll look at this book." What I started doing was actually making up my own ideas, because

what I found—I don't know if you noticed, when I played with Linda, this was my biggest criticism of my playing, that every riff she played, every run she played, I said, I've heard this before.

What she learned was basically a whole American idea of teaching jazz musicians. These are the scales, these are the riffs, this is Charlie Parker's solo and everyone knows Charlie Parker's solo. But Charlie Parker didn't do it like that. When he was playing, he didn't say, "I'm going to learn Coltrane's solo to play my solo," because he wanted to play *his own vibes*. So he got a good tape of John Patitucchi, one of the top bass players—he plays with Chick Corea, and his approach was this—you learn your scales and then instead of trying to find riffs that other musicians are playing—yea, that's cool—you can pick up ideas. Find your own, build up your own library of things to say from that, as opposed to trying to say what someone else said, which would be difficult, because you can't say the same thing that another musician has said. It's difficult. So it works easier that way. You say to someone, "Here's the C major scale." You give them ideas, and then they play around with some ideas and then they start to find their own little ideas from that.

MC: What you're saying fits so well with what Marc Seales, that jazz guy in my state (Seattle, Washington) was telling me. He says, "We jazz pianists practice our scales a hundred times. You classical people, you don't practice them enough. We do it so we can do things with it—make things with it."

BP: Yea, I think once you know it well enough, you've got to take what you want from it—because when Linda used to play it, I used to say, "You've got to play something else, because you're playing the same." It was because she was groomed with those riffs. They're teaching jazz like they teach classical music. This is the feeling I was getting, which shouldn't be. That's fine, but it shouldn't be like that. They've gotta make it more open, because the whole idea of jazz is to have more different people expressing different things. That's not happening if you're telling everybody—if you're locking everybody into a box like this.

MC: You know, that brings up an interesting thing. There's this new syllabus coming out of the UK that's a part of that British music education approach that's so rigid—that I'm sure Katrina and others have learned from—everybody taught the British way. I was so pleased because finally they're acknowledging jazz and they'll do exams in jazz in all these different levels. But the problem is, what you're just saying, everybody's going to be doing it the same way.

BP: It's going to be so structured.

MC: That's the problem. A wise teacher, of course, will do with it what you're suggesting—do it your own way. Use this just as a basis.

BP: Exactly. You just need the foundation of everything, and you've gotta try and find it. Some people will find it quicker, to say something; other people will take longer to say something. It's like learning a language in French class. Some people pick up, and some people take a few months before they really get it together. It's the same thing with music. The idea is, everyone has got to try and find their own way of saying something, otherwise it's not jazz, it's not. And you know, you get musicians saying, hey, play like so and so, play ...for what? Go and buy his CD, man. But we here in this country, we still have that problem— everyone saying play—like Richie plays saxophone so well. But guys are saying, play that David Sanborne...play like David Sanborne. Ah...that's depressing, man, to hear that. It's true, man, everyone should be saying—Richie, play like Richie—he's the man. Richie, not David Sanborne.

So we've gotta get away from that. That's why you get all the great musicians—they did that...and now everyone started copying those guys, so now we're back to square one. So what those musicians are trying to set up...everyone is bringing it back to square one again, which isn't the way.

You've heard Steve Coleman? When they asked him, how do you improvise, he said, "I go out in the garden and I watch a bee and flies and butterflies. That's how I want to play—the way those things fly." And that's the way he plays. When you hear those guys play, man, you think, is this guy playing in time, or what's he playing—because when a bee flies, it doesn't fly straight like this...you know? He flies this way, he goes, spins, does this...so this is how I want to play. I don't want to play things straight like that. You see, he had his own philosophy of saying, this is how I want to look at my improvisation, and he found it in the garden. So that worked for him.

Note from Bryan, April, 2005: "Now I'm in the UK playing some gigs with some jazz trios, mainly standards. This keeps me in touch as I'm now working a day job to pay the bills. I've been trying out a few projects, which involve African music with other locally based African musicians. I hope to get some recordings done of my music which is long overdue. Living here in the UK and trying to get your own style of music out is just as difficult, but at least there are some ways to try and solve various problems."

BUSI NCUBE

What I noticed most in listening to Busi's music, and in reading about her career, was the strong, rich, quality of her voice, and her ability to record in four different languages, Shona, Ndebele, Chewa and English. Busi is a vocalist and percussionist who has her own band, has made several CD's and has traveled widely with her band sharing her music. She incorporates a rainbow variety of musical influences in her calls for African renewal, and for laying down of guns and rebuilding. Busi's audiences are stirred to tap their feet and dance in response to her message.

The music itself consists of solo and group vocals in various languages often with close harmony, with the lyrics usually determining the rhythm, a strong beat, instrumental back-up using percussion, guitars, and synthesized sound, and call and response. Busi said that there is always movement and dance along with the music, as well as colorful costumes, which she designs for the performers. I wish I could have seen her perform but that was not possible in my limited time in Zimbabwe in 1999.

Busi is not only an accomplished musician, but also an active advocate for African women, especially women musicians, and a devoted wife and mother of two daughters. She has earned respect from her musical colleagues and is a credit to women in music. In the interview I found Busi to be very professional, yet down-to-earth. She seems to have a positive, proud sense of who she is and says so in an unassuming manner. Her way of answering my questions was direct and to the point, without much elaborating or storytelling, unless I pushed her in that direction.

Busi has commendable people skills as evidenced by the way she leads her band both musically and in business matters. She seems very aware of what makes her and her band loved by audiences—their diverse sounds resulting from the eclectic make-up of the group. Busi utilizes new ideas and sounds contributed by her band members, synthesizing it all into something cohesive that works musically. Her album, *African Renaissance*, is about Africa—the wars, hunger, diseases and corruption. Busi is a strong role model for young Zimbabwean women, especially women musicians.

Note: A friend of mine told me that Busi has a husband who is European, a dentist, who supports her music, both with approval and money.

I explained about the project and who some of the musicians were who I would be interviewing e.g., Chiwoniso Maraire. We talked about Chi's father, Dumisani Maraire, who had suddenly passed away, and what a shock it was. I mentioned several other musicians who would be in the book.

Myrna Capp: So let's start out with when you were born and where. What ethnic group and what influences?

Busi Ncube: I was born in Bulawayo. I was born in 1963, 15 June.

MC: Was yours a musical family?

BN: Yes. My father used to play township jazz in the 60's. *(Sunday Ncube, Busi's father, played township jazz; double bass and vocals, throughout Busi's childhood.)*
Note: When Busi was twelve, seven of the Ncube sisters sang as a choir, both in church and for traditional and other ceremonies. She played percussion and ngoma (Shona drum) also.

MC: So Joyce Makwenda would have studied him, your father?

BN: Yes, she actually produced some information about my father. She told me about the archives, and information from the archives about my father. Yes, it was very interesting. He's late (deceased).

MC: And your mother? Musical too?

BN: No. She wasn't. I have two sisters also, and they are in the business. One is in the U.K. She is doing basically music. And one is here with me. She's my twin sister, actually Pathie. She's with her own group, with her husband also, George, and she is also with me, so we're a bunch of musicians here.

MC: That's great. As far as learning to play instruments? And what about singing?

BN: Yea, singing. I have the talent, and my sister guided me. My sister, Doreen, she's older, she guided me most of the time, teaching me most of the tunes, because she'd been in the business already ten years before me. So I learned a lot from her. The first time I played with her in the same band, that was '82, I think, she was guiding me in how to do it.

We actually played in the same band. We were playing every day. We played for four days a week together—the band was.

MC: Did it work well, working with your sister?

BN: Yes, it worked well. Sometimes we used to fight a lot.

MC: Like when you would come back, would she say, "No I don't want you to do it that way?"

BN: Yea, she would.

MC: It was hard on you?

BN: Yea, sometimes. And she was particular. I learned a lot from her. She's in the U.K. now. She's far away. I go there quite often.

MC: Do you perform with her up there?

BN: Yes. The last gig we had there in London, we were playing at Africa Center together with other musicians that we picked up from there. They're Zimbabweans.

MC: So there's a big audience for Shona music up there?

BN: Yes, there is, and Ndebele. Zimbabwean music in general.

MC: Ok. Right. Sorry, I didn't mean to put you in the "Shona box."

BN: No, it's ok...it's alright.

MC: I'm admitting ...it's good you said that. And that makes a difference in some of the lyrics and all of that, doesn't it? (the fact that Busi is Ndebele)

BN: Yes, it does, a lot.

MC: Do you want to talk about that at all? Like what are your songs about? What inspires you when you write songs? Do you write songs?

BN: Yes I do. I write songs. All kinds from my background about where I come from, Bulawayo, how I grew up, and the way I'm living now. I grew up there. Most of my songs—I take them from my old songs. But now, because we are using everything modern, instruments and everything, the music sounds very different than earlier. Actually, because we were playing with a band, it was already changed.

MC: Did you do music in school?

BN: Yea. It was a choice. You had to choose whether you wanted to do it. It was not compulsory. I was interested in music. Mostly in school it was piano and choir.

MC: Oh, did you do some piano?

BN: Yes, we were doing some piano at Solucia Mission, a Seventh Day Adventist school, and choir singing.

MC: And solos, for you?

BN: Yes, yes, yes!

MC: So you had good experience in school.

BN: Yea, it was good.

MC: When it was time to be more on your own and not with your sister, how did you choose your group?

BN: Actually what I wanted was a recording band, and they were not recording at all during the time that I was there. I was still young and I wanted a group that I could record with, people that I could record with. Then I joined Ilanga.

MC: What is that?

BN: A band called Ilanga. It was a new band, and that's when I started my career, when I really started.

MC: What does Ilanga mean?

BN: Sun.

MC: Ndebele?

BN: Yea. So after that I recorded a lot of music. After that, I joined, after lots of the guys moved to South Africa. And Andy Brown, who came back, I played with him in the same band, and the late Don Gumbo; he was in South Africa. But after that we disbanded, and I formed my own group, which I'm still playing with, "Rain."

MC: And you're keeping busy?

BN: Yes, very, very busy. All over. Wherever we get the gigs and a good deal, we just go.

MC: Do you have a manager?

BN: Yes, we have a manager.

MC: Is that a necessary thing?

BN: It is, yes. Because I can't do everything. I can't do everything on my own, it's impossible.

MC: Does your manager help you with how tight to make your act, how your show is put together and how to change things when she/he thinks things aren't good enough?

BN: Yes. We always discuss it, and we have to always sit down and think about it with the other members of the group, and we find the best solution.

MC: So you kind of work it out in a democratic way?

BN: Yes, yes. And then monetary wise, it's always the most important part. We have to be straight about it.

MC: Do most of the people in your band have other ways of having income, or do they make their living in music?

BN: No, they only make their living in music.

MC: Oh. That's not easy, is it?

BN: It's very hard. It has to be really tight and we have to make sure that we have the jobs (gigs).

MC: What I have read about you is that you're really "up and coming" and doing things well.

BN: Now "they" are talking about "up and coming," but I'm not "up and coming" anymore, because I'm employing about twelve people, and I have a crew who need a source of income.

MC: This might be a hard question, but an interesting one. Each of the musicians that I've known, like Stella Chiweshe or Ephat Mujuru or obviously Albert Nyathi, they have something special. People want to go hear them for those reasons, you know? Something unique. What would you say, the kind of sound, or what is it that makes your group so popular, that people really want to pay attention to what you're doing? Is it the lyrics or something new?

BN: No, I'm not doing something new. I think it's the *sound*. My sound is very broad-based. I sing in four languages (Shona, Ndebele, Chewa and English), and I play different kinds of pieces, that are complex musically, and the lyrics are also. I think they're something that people like to listen to. They'll come and listen to it. There's somebody who plays mbira, it's unique, and we play African drum, and I play myself sometimes. I think that's what they enjoy, seeing me playing on the stage.

MC: Yes, that's a factor isn't it? I had several women on my list for this book project and I think maybe I will end up having about half men and half women, which I think is good. Maybe if I do another project like this I would just focus on women, because I think they need to be encouraged, don't you?

BN: Yea. They need a lot of encouragement.

MC: Do you find yourself encouraging women quite a bit?

BN: Yes, I do a lot, because I'm in this organization called Zimbabwe Women Musicians, which I established this last year. Yes, we launched it. It was what we really wanted to do, and it was going very well. Now the last show I did, when you came there (where I saw Busi in a meeting at a local club on an afternoon), I was organizing that, and it went very well. The people that came, the contribution, the musicians that it sponsored, it was great! It was a good thing, and I think will encourage them to do more. There is a project that we are planning, somebody that is coming, and said he was going to volunteer their services for me to coordinate the women, to record their music for free, and so it's very good.

MC: That kind of focus here in Zimbabwe, from the things I've read, is needed. The women need a lot of encouragement.

BN: A *lot* of encouragement.

MC: It's very tough. And a lot of times they are the ones that are the victims of the AIDS problems.

BN: Yes, it is so sad. It's a big problem. They need a lot of encouragement, and sometimes they just give up because there's nothing they think that they can do. You can't fight in this. You are always stepped upon, so it's pointless for them to raise their heads, you know? There's no room.

MC: But, I've also been reading that in the liberation struggle, women played a key role. So obviously women can do a lot.

BN: They did…a lot!

MC: Do you feel that music, even songs you write can play a role?

BN: Yea, I think so.

MC: Have you written any songs with those kinds of lyrics?

BN: I've written a lot of songs that address women's issues. Most of my stuff is about women. I've always got another woman in mind, or the uplifting of women, the stronger they are the better.

MC: Do you get women in your audiences giving you good feedback? Comments?

BN: Yes, yes. Even the last time—the trip I had, when I told you I was going away, it was a woman that pushed me, wanted to do this. It's very good. I went to Sweden. Yes, it was youth from Sweden and Zimbabwean youth who have been working together. It was a ten-year jubilee, so they wanted us from Zimbabwe. The audience was very enthusiastic, and it was a pity, I brought some CD's. I brought about ten, and I didn't realize what kind of response I would get, and they were bought in one show, and I had no more to sell. I was thinking, I wish I could get somebody to send me more CD's, but it was too late. I'm still going to send some.

MC: So is your goal to travel around like that more, or are you content to be here?

BN: No, I want to travel around. It's always an experience. It's always exciting. Meet new people, new ideas.

MC: Exactly. There are some other things that I want to ask you about. I did a project at the University of Washington. In fact that's when I went to some classes with Dumi Maraire. He was in a program there too. I teach class piano where we have electronic pianos with earphones and people who play non-keyboard instruments—they all want to learn some piano. And I just have to add this, Ephat wants to learn piano, Stella wants to. They say, if you're coming back you must teach us piano.

BN: Yes, it's very good because the musicians, the ones that are playing, they don't have any idea about theory. They didn't have a chance to do theory. They did theory *practically,* because they played naturally. They play mbira, and naturally we played drums. Naturally we sing. So for most of the people, music education wasn't possible because the College of Music was too expensive. They couldn't get access. Now, Saturday's, we, at the College of Music, do workshops, and those workshops are for free. Now students are paying a minimal fee, because it's not being sponsored now. It was being sponsored by one NGO (non-governmental organization) at one time, and I was doing it. I did it for some time, but it was taking my time. Also, I was teaching there for some time, every Saturday, but it was taking so much of my time. I was playing on Fridays, and then Saturday I have to wake up in the morning at ten, and I would have come home at 5:00 a.m. So it was straining me so much. I didn't have time to spend with my children and my husband. It was taking so much of my time. I did it for awhile and then the second time they called, I said, "I can't do it because it's really straining my life."

It's a very good thing. I would do it if it was any other time like, maybe one evening a week or so. I would do it, but it's Saturday morning. I used to do it every Saturday morning. I would wake up at 10. It's too much for me. It really encourages everyone involved because there's no age limit. I had all ages in my class—all ages from the smallest up.

MC: What I was leading up to is, I'm very interested in improvisation. I am a classical pianist, where we had to learn everything from notation, and you had to memorize it, and then I got interested in improvisation, playing by ear, and I started reading what jazz musicians do. You use your ear more, because you take that page away and see what you can do. So I started trying that with my piano students and of course they had problems. They had never done that, so it was very difficult for them. Now, all my students—I teach them to play by ear. I started Ephat—the other day we had a few minutes, so he was learning, "O When the Saints Come Marching In." He was excited because he could immediately start playing the melody and put some chords with it, quite easily. It will take him longer to learn how to read, but he wants to do it—learn to read—to open up some things.

BN: It does a lot, it does open up some things, because when you don't have that skill you don't expand. Your ear can only take you so far.

MC: So for your own children, if you encourage them in music, you would encourage them to learn to read?

BN: Yea, I would encourage them to learn to read and play also. I would encourage them. I will teach them physically to read, to learn to play.

MC: Are they learning music now?

BN: Yes they are. I was in a school concert, the school concert in the big school here down the road, it was beautiful. Yea, singing.

MC: So do you hope they'll learn to play instruments too?

BN: Yea, I hope so. I won't push it. I'll just let them do what they enjoy.

MC: Were you pushed when you were a child?

BN: No, never. I was never pushed.

MC: You just came to play because you wanted to?

BN: I wanted it. I wanted it so much, I loved it so much. Everything I did, like singing. I used to entertain the whole school and when they found out that I have made a career in music, they were not surprised, because I used to entertain in the dormitory. I used to entertain everywhere. Just go there and start singing.

MC: So you were a natural?

BN: Yea.

MC: That's great. Now when you write songs, some of it is probably the same every time you sing it, but there are some things you do to it, you improvise, you play around with the material, right?

BN: Yes, I do a lot.

MC: Could you talk about how you decide what to do, how does it come to you? What gets you going when you're improvising?

BN: It's like, the music that I've been playing for a long time, I just get this feeling that I want to improvise, you feel it. Sometimes it's the audience also that encourages you. You cannot communicate with some audiences, they are so far away. Sometimes you give more to people that you feel you are in contact with. You give more, you open up. I always try new things.

MC: Now "ulalation," a vocal technique unique to certain places in Africa, that's pretty common? Do you do it different ways?

BN: No, there's always basic, but I try with my voice to do new things, I'm always trying to.

MC: Do you, as far as your group, do you kind of get each other excited, kind of nourish each other?

BN: Yes, we do all different things. Always there's something new on stage. We really encourage each other, and mostly it's communica-

tion, you know? You have to communicate when you're on stage—you are playing together and the group knows when I'm feeling something, e.g., (Busi sings an idea: "a-pic-a, a-pic-a") so they know you can go improvise. There is always communication and we encourage each other. We don't even say anything, they know it. If you look at somebody, you can see that they are all going to follow the idea.

MC: That reminds me of what I was reading about jazz musicians—"taking their solos," that's the way you say it in jazz.

BN: It's the same.

MC: What would you call the kind of music you do?

BN: I call it, I don't have a real specific name. This is mbira music and so on, because I do all kinds of different music. I do mbira music, I do my own music, I mix the rhythms from Africa, African rhythms that I get from the other countries in Africa. It's always different and it's like a rainbow. I like to call it "rainbow music."

MC: How important is dance, or movement, in what you do?

BN: Very, very important.

MC: So you include some of that?

BN: Very important, yes. I include a lot of dance, because I'm moving most of the time, not standing in one place, because most of the music is very danceable.

MC: Like you *have* to dance to it, right?

BN: Yes, and I enjoy it. I make my own choreography.

MC: What about the costumes? Who decides about those?

BN: The costumes I do myself also and just take it to somebody to do it for me, but I design them. I make sure of that.

MC: If you have any brochures of that sort of thing, I would love to see those too. And, like I said before, I wish so much we could see you perform, and then my daughter could photograph you in the costumes because that adds so much too, I think. Can you think of anything else that I should have asked you, and that you would like to say?

BN: Maybe about what was the most exciting time in my life, my career, and what I've achieved so far?

MC: That would be really good.

BN: Yes, the most exciting time was...you know, you get excited and you're scared and you are so excited, and you think, "Wow!" There was a concert for human rights here in Zimbabwe and they were going to sell out, because all the biggest artists you can think of, all of them, Peter Gabriel, Chet Mann, Yosando, you didn't expect it to be like—we are not sure whether this is Zimbabwe. These celebrities came in for that concert, and that was it, they never came back. You know they were there, it was amazing! It was like an international event. I was starting the group, and we were the biggest group there, and we shared the stage with them. Afterwards all the actors held hands and we were as one, with each one in the audience. We were so excited, yea, yea, yea!

MC: Sounds like quite an honor!

BN: Yea, it was. You never see them again, and I don't think I'll share the stage with them again. It was really a big, big, crowd! Yes, I think that was the most exciting. Then my recordings—so far I think I've done about seven albums.

MC: That's quite a lot.

BN: Yes, seven albums, and I think I did four with Delana and three with others.

MC: You're doing very well. You're not that old.

BN: I'm trying to keep up.

MC: Do you want to say anything about your dreams or vision for the future? Would it just be more of the same, or do you want it to take a different turn?

BN: What I would like mostly is if I could be able to sell the music internationally.

MC: So everybody around the world would know? And appreciate it?

BN: Yea, and *appreciate it!*

rs, Zimbabwe, 2000

STELLA CHIWESHE

Mesmerizing music, an elegant, mystical-spiritual quality to her performances, a theatrical, dramatic presence on stage, stunning outfits, elaborate headwear or hairstyles and intense absorption in what she is doing sum up Stella Chiweshe's performances. I first saw and heard her in the "Global Divas" concert in Seattle where she was billed as "The Mbira Queen of Zimbabwe," along with Susan Baca from Peru, and Tish Hinojosa from South Texas. The next time I heard her perform was in Harare at the Book Café with her band which included mbira, hosho, marimbas, percussion, guitar, vocals and dance.

Although Stella enjoys being the central focus in performance, she said that she has learned to enjoy working with her band in collaboration. They know when to stay in the background and allow Stella to respond to her inner voices, which always speak to her. Is this improvisation? I think so. It was clear to me that Stella is wise about how to broaden her own and her group's appeal and how to market her music. When my photographer took photos of Stella, she varied her hairdo, used interesting poses, and wore an eye-catching outfit that enhanced her image, giving her a unique sense of "style." Stella was sensitive to mixing/fusion in her music as evidenced by the instrumentation in her group e.g., use of Zimbabwean and Western instruments, and the wide variety of musical repertoire they performed.

There was an otherworldly side to Stella that made me wonder what it would be like to interview her. But sitting in her lounge and visiting her was a pleasure. She rather enjoyed telling me the stories of her life, opening up and revealing some of her inner self that proved to be fascinating. Stella has a vital connection to the past, because she grew up in rural Zimbabwe, where the missionaries and the white government banned traditional Shona mbira music. This still appalls Stella! She knows that traditional music is important and must be preserved.

She was determined to play mbira as a girl, in spite of the obstacles, namely, that children, and especially girls and women, should not play mbira. Because of the gender inequality and discrimination in traditional Shona culture against women, Stella is adamant about promoting women musicians and has become an activist. She is an inspiration to women musicians in Zimbabwe and around the world.

Stella is married to a German man and spends time in Germany regularly. Although she did not mention it, this connection certainly has helped in the cultural brokering of her as a performer, and in dissemination of her recordings. She has better access to recent technology, broader audiences and global media than many Zimbabwean musicians have

She told me "the rhythm that grew inside her," which started when she was a child, changed to a burning desire. She thinks "everybody should let out their inner voice" as she has. She had a special way of describing certain things. Her explanation of how she finds "her place" in any music she hears, was intriguing as well as puzzling. It sounded like her own kind of improvisation to me.

Myrna Capp: The kinds of things I'm interested in are, what your life has been from the time you were young, as a musician. Your stories?

SC: Since I was a young girl, I had a rhythm inside me that was always with me and this rhythm, I was imitating it on everything that could make sound, and this sound grew up with me. What I liked to do most was to sing. I grew up with my grandparents, my mother's parents, and my best position to relax was with my *head down!*

MC: Maybe we should have a photograph with your *head down*.

SC: My grandmother was always worried about how I could really do that, but if everybody was sitting, my head was down, and I felt quite comfortable with that. And about my singing, I didn't want to make noise for people. I wanted to go far away from the ears of the people. In the old days, people were not as many as these days. When I go to the area where I grew up, where we used to herd cattle, or where there was a field, now there are houses. It was in Mhondoro. I was born in 1946 on the 8th of July. I always asked my grandfather when it was our turn to go and herd cattle, because the Shona people used to take turns to herd the cattle for two or three days. I always asked my grandfather to go far away from the people so that I could sing as loud as I could.

He never asked me why, he never got worried about it. My grandfather was so nice to me. Where I grew up we were under the rule of the missionaries and the mission had a very big area; the people under the mission were called Christians, who were not allowed to sing traditional African songs. So, while growing up, I never heard a traditional song, only church songs. And as children we were told to run away from people who belonged to the heathens, e.g., traditional Zimbabweans. People who played the mbira and drums were kicked out of the community.

Traditional African musicians needed to go and live far away, so that if the drums are loud, the Christians could not hear them, so that's why we were told to always watch out for those people. If we saw them, we were to run away from them, and to report it to the mission, that they passed our area. So today, I am the person who I was told to run away from! And this sound that grew up with me, I do not know what it was, but today I know that sound of the drum. I'd never seen a drum before, and I've not forgotten the sound, the rhythm that was in there. When I was eight years old, my mother took me from her parents, to go and look after the young baby. She was living in Masenbura, far from Mhondoro. It's near Bindura. The people there were living far from the church, so that's where I first heard mbira. I was eight years old. Children of my age were not allowed to go to listen to drums and to mbira, and I think it was because they were afraid, not interested, I don't know.

But one day when I was playing mbira I saw something that made me know why the children are not allowed. I saw the elders of the people who were possessed. They were taller than how they were, very tall. And I think that's the reason why, because children see what we cannot see. One day my mother was preparing supper earlier, and I was wondering why she was all excited, and she told me that it was because it was a mbira day, to go and listen to these. And I asked her, what is mbira, and she said you've nothing to do with that, so I had nothing to do with that, but I was going to go with her. She tried to stop me, but it was not possible. I followed her and when I entered the door trying to get in, all of the people were shocked, surprised why my mother had let me come along. And my mother told them that she had tried her best to stop me. They could also try to take me out, and there was this man who tried to come and lift me out and take me outside. I was famous for screaming. I screamed loudly, and I told them that I was not going to disturb them. I really was sitting behind the door in a way that I was not going to disturb them, and they allowed me to stay.

Then the whole thing started, the Bira, and the people started to dance. They were enjoying it very much, but I did not get the rhythm, so that kept me going again and again, and by that time they were used to my presence, so I started to go wherever the elders were going. It was only a few times when I could join the kids of my age, but when I did that, joined the kids of my age, to go out in the moonlight and sing and dance, for me they were not singing properly. They were not responding to the one who was singing and they were making a small circle. I was always going behind the circle and started to sing alone and clap for myself and dance at the same time. Then the people would say, let's join her, and then I was giving them orders. If you want to join you have to make a big circle, everybody has got to sing, everybody has got to clap, and dance. I grew up like that. I didn't want anybody in my circle until today when I'm on stage. I wanted the whole dance for myself.

And if somebody tries to come in to dance, I say, ok, just for a short time, and remember that it's not his dancing place, or her dancing place. So it grew up with me and that was only three years from the time I started to know the man playing mbira. Three years. When I first saw him I was age nine or ten. When I was 17, I saw a group of mbira players that are playing today, and for the first time I spent the whole night playing hosho for them, and the people were surprised how I could play hosho so well. I had never played hosho before. But it was because of the force of the rhythm that grew up with me. It's really easy. It's one, two, three, four. You learned to play?

MC: Well yes, I've done it and I can do it, but it's so easy to get thrown off by other things that are going on.

SC: The trick really of playing hosho is to imagine that you are the seeds that are inside. Go inside with your mind and see them and don't be taken by anything that is around you. Then think of—you can close your eyes too. Because if you watch the people who are dancing... just close your eyes and imagine you are the seeds that are inside, and you just go. You have to listen to one note that is coming continuously. That is what you follow. Because if you listen to all the keys, then you'll get lost. Just one key.

MC: See, as a pianist, I'm used to following all the different voices going on. I do a lot of accompanying so, as a pianist you have to listen to all the different things going on, but what you're saying makes a lot of sense for hosho. That's interesting. I like it when you talk about those things that are going on in your mind when you're playing or when you're practicing. Those things are very interesting to me. Now you write songs, don't you?

SC: Yes, sometimes.

MC: For your performances, how do you get inspired to write a song?

SC: What happens is that I hear voices and I just pass the voices. The voices come (she whispers) and when the voices come, the guys who play with me have learned that I hear voices and I hear sounds. When the sound comes, I stop them and they've got to stop quickly so that I give them the song, or I give them the words, before they pass and then it goes on like that. When it is finished, then my part comes. When I'm dancing I am like one of the instruments. So my part is just to fill in the gap. I find this gap in every type of music in this world. When I listen to that, I just find my part is vacant.

MC: Talk about that some more. I'm curious to know more about that.

SC: I meant to say, if I listen to a CD, or if I go to watch a show I always find my place. Yes, I always find my place.

MC: I see, there's something for you there—a place to fill in.

SC: Yes.

MC: So for you, that's a kind of improvisation isn't it? For you to be a part of it? Maybe like jazz? Because they're always looking for a place to fill in, too?

SC: I don't struggle to find a part. I just feel it, I hear it.

MC: So does that happen when you hear some jazz, or some gospel, or some blues even, there's a place there?

SC: It is. There's a place there for me.

MC: So when you turn on a CD and you're doing some things vocally, or you've got your hosho, you're doing some things? Or is it mostly in your head?

SC: It's mostly in my head, but I see that if I do this, it will fit in together with that, and with all types of music that we have in this world. Every type of music has got its place. So you know, not to own the musics that are played around the world is nice for everyone. Some music is really boring. But before you really say it's boring, find where it belongs in you.

You only have to open up and not get bored, because if you get bored by other musics, you can be seen standing up in a full theatre and going out because you are bored.

MC: What kind of concerts do you like to go to? Where you know you will not get bored? Do you go to concerts?

SC: I don't, No.

MC: Do you go to clubs around here?

SC: No, I don't go anywhere.

MC: You listen to music, though?

SC: I don't. No. I have a radio there and I don't even switch it on.

MC: Is it because you have so much music going on in your head?

SC: I do. When I'm driving, I've got so many things to think of and to do. I like music that is sentimental music, like piano music, classical music. It cools me down. I don't like this music that is very hard with really...(she makes some sounds).

MC: That is very interesting. Since I'm a classical pianist, especially, I'm intrigued with that. I find that, for me, classical piano is a kind of a therapy often times. So that makes some sense.

SC: You know, I played somewhere (Dutch...somewhere in the Netherlands) and there was a lady who came to tell me after the show. She has been listening to jazz a lot and she told me not to go anywhere because she was going home to collect all her CD's and to give them to me. She wanted to listen to just mbira. Then she brought all the CD's that she used to listen to, to me and then I just gave her back one mbira CD and she was happy and she said she was going to listen to that again and again and again.

MC: When you were in Seattle you had some other musicians with you. Do you prefer when you perform to have a group with you? Or do you like to perform alone?

SC: I like both. Alone is very nice and also very relaxed. I don't have anybody to say I will do this or to make a program. Like when you're driving with a trailer, when you're turning you've got to be careful of your trailer. But then, sometimes I miss them too, because when we were four, then there would be three mbira and a hosho, and then sometimes two mbira, hosho and ngoma (Shona drum). And I like it also sometimes with the band. In my band I have two marimbas, a soprano and alto, bass and tenor, and drum kit and mbira.

MC: It's a very different kind of sound, isn't it?

SC: Yea, it's a bigger sound and gives me a lot of energy to dance.

MC: I was just going to ask you, what about the dance part of it? How do you feel about that? How important is it to include some dance?

SC: I like it for dancing. Then I can really explode because I have a lot of support.

MC: So the body movement part of what you do is really quite important. Does it come out of the instrumental music or the vocal music or do they all just kind of fit together. How does that work? I read about that. For instance, we were watching Ephat and his son and another guy doing a performance last week, and it seemed like the instrumental music was just great, but then when somebody got up there and started dancing it seemed more complete.

SC: Yes, where all the instruments are there and I stand up to dance, I feel if I am around the instruments too, how my feet are dancing is rather a *fill-up* that should be there.

MC: That's good. I like that. This whole idea of musical talent in your culture, let's talk about that. You're Shona, right?

SC: Yes.

MC: Some of the cultures that I've read about in my studies don't really think of musical talent the way that we do in the West, where some child prodigies like Mozart are very gifted in music from the time they're very young. How is it in Shona culture? I mean, obviously you started responding and needing to do music from the time you were very young. What if a child didn't have that urge but maybe showed some promise, would the parents encourage them? How is musical talent encouraged or developed in Shona culture?

SC: Most of the parents think that music is something that is not a career, that a *child* goes for. They think that music will really disturb the child from doing other things, from learning. I don't know where that came from. I think that it has got a root somewhere. I don't know where.

MC: I've read things that fit very well with what you just said. Also the whole thing of women doing music, and I sense from people I've talked to and things I've read, that women are really coming out and doing music like they never did in the past, and I know you're a supporter of that, very much.

SC: I think that is a root from the jealousies of the men. Because the men, they think that if a woman is doing that, singing and dancing, this is *way out*. To sing and dance, and most of the time it's done in the evenings when men think women should be in their homes with their families, and this is where it comes from.

MC: Is that starting to change? Being more open for women, and not so much jealousy, or do you think that's just there, and it's very difficult to break that down?

SC: No, it is our families. It's really there, but I think people are starting to fight hard, because music is needed everywhere, at a funeral, at church, when you're putting a baby to sleep, everywhere, for yourself. It's needed and it should be known, and it should be encouraged, if somebody wants to sing.

MC: Absolutely! Kristin, my daughter here, is wanting to focus on women and children in Zimbabwe, in her photography. The more I'm thinking about women in music, and the tradition of women not being in music so much, I'm wishing there were a way to help with that. Maybe interviewing more women is good. I'm glad that I'm doing Busi and Chi and yourself.
(Stella suggested I contact Virginia Changano and Irene Chigamba. Virginia is with a band called Harare Mambos)

SC: If you go through Virginia's husband, he allows her to sing, but he does not allow that her name is out somewhere.

MC: It's a problem.

SC: Yea. If she composes a song or does anything it's just called the "Harare Mambos."

MC: How do you feel about that?

SC: It's really painful. (I mentioned Chi Maraire and Andy Brown and Stella said...) I just heard from the agencies and the promoters saying they should try more. They are just kids who are starting. They'll come up. And I like that Chi kept singing, because I saw her when she was about ten or so, and she was singing, but when I meet her, I'll ask her if she has this recording where she was young. Her parents were very nice because they encouraged her. She was so lucky, you know? I feel very sorry for her. Now she doesn't have a father; her mother passed away, now her father.

MC: It's difficult for her. Do you know Claire Jones?

SC: Yea.

MC: She was telling me today that they put Chi in the hospital just today, because she's pregnant, you know? They thought she really needed some rest, so they put her in the hospital for four days. It's too much stress I think right now. Many people have been coming to their home to pay their respects, which is very nice. But it takes so much energy.

SC: Yes, for a young girl like Chi. It's too much for her.

MC: So I'm going to be very careful. If it's too much I won't interview her. Maybe a telephone interview later or something. I don't want to add to her stress. I appreciate you sharing that because I kind of wondered about that. She seems so young. Dumi and I were good friends. We were in a class together at the University of Washington and then I studied some mbira with him. Then we were in his home for dinner five years ago when we were here, and so we had quite a bit of connection. It's hard to lose someone who is a friend.

SC: I was shocked.

MC: I think we all were. I want to change the subject just a bit and go back to something I was reading in that book by Fred Zindi about your being so popular in Germany and in Europe, and not appreciated very much in Zimbabwe. I was wondering, is that changing now, would you say?

SC: The reason is as I told you, that we grew up in a situation that we were told to run away from people like me, and this went very deep into other people. What I do is not something that can be easily appreciated, so that is the reason.

MC: Ok. But now in Zimbabwe it seems like they're accepting what you are doing more.

SC: Yes, because you know, I fight very hard. I pushed so hard and I think I inspired a lot of other women, and wherever I go people know me.

MC: You're famous.

SC: Yea, but I don't take it as though it's me who is famous. It's mbira. Mbira is famous now. You know mbira was not allowed, first of all and you could be arrested, you know? To be found with mbira. You couldn't walk around with mbira. That was not allowed. You would just go to jail without any questions, nothing, because you were found with mbira. It was like that. It was really very hard.

First of all, the first missionaries who came here knew how powerful our culture was. I can say anybody's culture is very powerful. Then they told the people that that belonged to a certain ? ; a mistake that the people have been doing the whole of their lives. They should just stop to do all that, and start to do something else, you know? And some people agreed to that, and then after that it was the government. For me it was really confusing because if it was not allowed by God, and is the government arresting because God does not like it? Then I started to watch, to learn mbira, all the people, men and women were against that I wanted to learn mbira. It was so hard. They were talking. A lot of whites failed to stop me, but everything that they said gave me courage.

First of all, there were the missionaries and then the government and then the people. What was going on I had to learn, because I wanted to listen to mbira whenever I wanted to, and I could not be stopped, because I really had a burning desire inside me. *That rhythm that grew up with me changed into a burning desire.* I wanted to play, and the day that I was told to sit down and be taught by the whites, I felt it leaving me. So nothing could stop me.

MC: No wonder it happens like it does on the stage then. You have to do it! It's kind of exciting to hear you say it that way. Do you want to add anything at all that I might have left out that you think is important before I turn the tape recorder off?

SC: What I think is important is that people should always let out the *inner voice*, because everybody's got an *inner voice* that says something, or that is saying something, and people are always oppressing it, you know? It's really not nice.

babwe, 1999

Harare, 2000

Harare, 1999

ALBERT NYATHI

Interviewing Albert Nyathi sitting on the bleachers of the huge soccer stadium outside Harare, with birds squawking overhead, and soccer players shouting signals and whooping, was unusual, to say the least. It was distracting! But as the interview proceeded, I was drawn into Albert's story-telling. He saw himself as a simple herd boy who happened to like words and poetry. He happened to be good at reciting (public recitation), first at school, and later for all kinds of audiences, including important State events, where the Presidents of Zimbabwe and South Africa were present.

His ability to improvise so-called "praise poetry" was impressive to those around him, he discovered, to his surprise. When he realized that physically and mentally he could only do his recitations for a limited part of a performance, he wisely added music and dance, which broadened his appeal.

Albert courageously addressed politically sensitive issues about which he cared deeply, in spite of the fact that this openness is not currently acceptable to the government in Zimbabwe. His sense of humor and willingness to "tell tales" on himself was refreshing. Albert used a traditional presentation style (dramatic, oral recitation) to convey very current content in his performances. At times "praise" is/was a misnomer for what he did. He was actually criticizing and poking at issues and people, but could get away with it because of the traditional mode of presentation.

Albert's passion for helping talented youthful musicians to become recognized and known was admirable. To him it was a calling. Because much of the thrust of his performances was through language (Shona and Ndebele) I wonder how well he would be accepted outside of Zimbabwe and South Africa. We talked of his coming to the U.S., where he would need to orient his praise song presentations to appeal to very different audiences. However, I believe that Albert, with his fluency in English, would bring important global concerns about Africa to the U.S. through his poetry, and would entertain brilliantly (as the British would say) in his own unique way.

Myrna Capp: What I'm looking for are some interesting things that may come out of the questions. I have a few questions prepared, and for you I have some different kinds of questions, since you've been called a "Praise Poet."

Albert Nyathi: It's a pity. I don't know why I'm called that. That's just a fusion of music and poetry and dance.

MC: You seem to be different than a lot of the other musicians in that the poetry part, the words, are much more important than for some of these artists that are doing music. I'm just wondering how that happened? What kind of a background did you come out of?

AN: Well I was born in a little hut in the countryside in 1962, November 15th precisely. And I grew up there as a herd boy, herding cattle and goats, starting with goats of course. And I lived the kind of life that you'd find in the countryside. As boys would fight, beat each other, you'd not report at home that you'd been beaten. You'd rather say that you fell on a tree or something. If you said you were beaten by some other boy, your father would in turn, beat you up, saying, "How did that happen? You must be brave, you must be strong, you can't just be beaten by other little boys, you must be strong." That's how I grew up. Education at that time was not very important. People would go—my brothers would go down to South Africa and work in the mines, and they'd bring back for themselves bicycles and a radio, and they'd buy a table and four chairs and so on and so forth, and a bed, and that was good. And they would buy their kettle. For us, agriculture was more important. Therefore there was no example of one who had gone to school and succeeded in the community because of education.

So we could only see success through those who had gone to South Africa and worked in the mines; that's how I grew up. I used to run away from school. I didn't like school at all. I would hide somewhere when others came from school. I was with my cousin when we heard others talk, coming from school. We would just move in front of them and pretend we were also coming from school, until one day we were caught in that kind of scenario, and we were beaten up thoroughly by the headmaster. That's the kind of life I lived when I was young. Apparently my life was more a South African life than Zimbabwean. When I grew up I never knew anything called Shona.

It was in the countryside in Matabeleland, in Gwanda, to be specific. In Gwanda the radio stations that we listened to mainly were South African. For instance, even today Zimbabwean Broadcasting Corporation is nowhere to be found. I mean, there is very little of it. It's much better now, but there used to be nothing, so I never used to know there was anything called Shona when I grew up. I knew Ndebele and Sotho, in that area only, nothing more. Therefore I only knew of Shona in about 1976 (I was born in '62,) and that's about 14 years. That's when I started knowing about Shona, in 1976. I found out that there is a thing called Shona. The music that I listened to was South African and that had a lot of influence on me. But, besides, the language that I speak is Ndebele, which is Zulu, which is Swati, which is Xhosa. These Nguni language people have a specific type of music, it's very much related, more or less the same. It's all from similar cultural backgrounds. They were one people, the Ngwani, the Zulu, the Ndebele, the Xhosa, they are called the Nguni group of languages, and if I go to South Africa today, or to Swaziland, I'll be able to communicate without a single problem. It's like Americans can speak English and understand it, even though there are various versions of English. It's the same.

MC: So how is this impacting you, being here in Zimbabwe? You have all of that South African influence, language and everything. Why are you here? Why are you doing your music for Shona people, especially?

AN: Oh, here in Harare in particular? Well I think I also deserve to be called Zimbabwean because my people came here in the 1860's.

MC: Your people have been here a long while!

AN: Yea, and some people in South Africa, when I get to South Africa, they say, but how come you speak Zulu? I say, it's not Zulu, it's Ndebele and they say, no, this is old Zulu. I say, no, it is Ndebele. For sure I consider myself Zimbabwean, and I and my people are here as well.

MC: Now when you do your songs, and the language—the poetry, is so important, all this background is there and it is informing what you're doing. Like the topics that you sing about, that your poetry is about, are they about things that are important in Zimbabwe now, or is the history important too? What about that?

AN: Well as far as I'm concerned, history is very important in my life, and perhaps in every one else's life, because it tells us of yesterday. We have to know about yesterday to understand today, and to have a vision for tomorrow. That's how important I consider history, and therefore I do not leave out that element, of history. I use history as an aspect in my work. In my work, the content is what is happening now, and what is possibly going to happen tomorrow. But the *form*, my *form*, is very much a traditional one.

Here I'm talking of the actual presentation, the way I present my works. Let me use the word "steal." I very much steal from the past in terms of form, in terms of presentation. But the content is what surrounds me today. There has always been a problem. I studied literature and I know that some European critics, English poetry or literature critics might not consider African literature the same as other literature. They say African literature is protest literature, and I say, while I agree, I'm saying no, you can't dismiss it as protest literature simply. If protest means dismissal then I don't take the point. But if it adds weight to the argument that it is still literature, then I agree. I'm talking of the content. There is no way I can be among burning issues, and the issues are burning, while I'm writing about the roses. I'll write about my nature, my situation, and my current situation. My situation and content indicates that I'm "burning," that's why I talk of my content as current.

In other words we look at our current situation and say, this is where we come from, this is where we are, this is where we are possibly going. Some people then have taken me to be a political musician-poet, if you like, but I've said that, no, if politics means, going to the butcher or to the grocer, and finding bread has gone up by forty percent, and I sing about it, and you consider that to be politics, then I am political! So in my works I talk, I sing, I do poetry and chant about what is happening currently. But I started this whole thing just as a poet, a stage poet, performing. And as I was young, I could not really write. When I was young, at primary school, secondary school, I could not write. I used to perform praise poetry at school (Albert performed a brief example of the poetry for the interview).

Eventually I started writing. The short piece (the one he just performed) is Shaka Zulu. That's one aspect that you should know, that we come from some kind of kingdoms, from a monarch whose culture has been praised, that's why we say praise. But it means "praise" in quotes because I'm attacking through that praise. Initially I couldn't write when I was at school, and I used to compose and recite traditional poetry. Then eventually I started writing, and during opening, prize-giving days, at all schools that I went to, I used to recite. The headmaster would invite me, the staff would invite me to write something and recite, and I used to recite. Then when I came up to Harare in 1988, I continued that tradition. There is a group, I think it is called "New Dawn," but I already had one group.

MC: A local one?

AN: No, it was from England. It was playing on Radio One. I heard them on Radio One, they were fusing poetry with music. I heard them in '88, I think. I heard it and I really enjoyed that. There was music in what they were doing. Then initially there had been someone called Cosmopita, from South Africa, who was an exile, and he was a mentor to young poets. He would read for us and he would teach us how to read poetry to make it more interesting, more exciting. And we even had shows with him, and I admired him a lot. Cosmopitas, he's edited a few plays in South Africa. He's a member of Parliament now in South Africa. I hope I could meet him and he sees how far I've gone. Previously he had done that, but when I heard this group, "New Dawn," I then started seeing the possibility of fusing poetry and music.

With poetry I can go for thirty minutes and it's still interesting, on stage, non-stop, working, showing, talking, but it's very demanding. I fuse things in order for it to be thirty minutes. I do it with storytelling. There's a story that I do alone on stage, I go for thirty minutes. The story is about 15 minutes, the poetry is about 15 minutes. But I realized that I wanted to entertain more. Then in 1990 I grouped with someone named Titus Mutzare and Cynthia Mungoza and we called ourselves "Alcyti Poets," Al for Alfred, Cy for Cynthia, and Ti for Titus—Alcyti Poets. Then we got a group called Badzimba, and they played some traditional Shona stuff and we went on for quite some time. But Cynthia went to Australia to do her masters degree and Titus is a lawyer by training, so he has a company called African Communications. Me, I continued. But I joined the Arts Council. I happened to be the most willing. Others who had joined me, one by one, started seeing no vision in it. But I had a vision, I had a dream!

MC: You're like America's Martin Luther King, Jr.

AN: So, I went on and I worked for the National Arts Council as Publications and Information officer. As I worked, it was a bit difficult because I went to Denmark for six months, I went to Sweden, and I went to Holland three times. It was difficult. I was working hard. Now they made me acting Director of the National Arts Council of Zimbabwe. I worked for three months and I saw it couldn't work. I'm not a bureaucrat. Eventually I quit, realizing I needed to. Because there's a board, you see, and I was merely an employee, as acting Director, and each time I suggested things, they were not taking them up. I had been fighting for a Cultural Center, a Cultural Academy, and they've been doing nothing. Eventually, on February 28th, 1999, I said, you're not taking my ideas, there's lots of money lying around,

if you go to Danida. Our people are artistic if given a place where we can rehearse, exhibit, and so on, but you talk of these things since 1980, and I don't think there's any vision in you. I'm sorry, bye bye. And I quit. And then I got into music fulltime. Here at Itimbo Studios. That's where we rehearse. That's where we get youngsters from all over to come, like the one's you saw, those guys (we heard a group when we came to meet Albert).

MC: So you like working with kids?

AN: Yea, I do.

Grayson Capp: Do you ever go back to your village? Do you ever go back to where you were born? Do you ever visit?

AN: Yea, I was there three weeks ago, but I came from Hawaii. Because I'd been to Libya, South Africa, then I went to Hawaii because I got so tired. Hawaii was good because I could swim, swim, swim, although I didn't know how to swim. They managed to teach me a little. Having traveled that much I felt tired. Coming from there I went straight home. You can still "breast feed," you know, as a grown up. You can still breast feed from your mother (be nourished by her), so I went to breast feed.

GC: That's what I wondered, if you went back sometimes just to get away from it all.

AN: I do when I do quite a lot of traveling. I buy a car, a car different than the one I had previously. I would go down to the village and show it to my parents and to the villagers, who would have some snuff to wish it well, and pour a bit of beer on it (local rituals).

MC: And they think you're doing well, very successful with this new car, huh?

AN: Yea, but they don't like it. I've got a message of, they're not as happy as when I buy a truck. A truck for them is more important, when you go down to the village. Actually, I was inexperienced. My sisters and cousins, who are married, from the city, when we go down, and there's a function, and they see me, they think, ah, this is good man, it's a sign of success. But the villagers don't think that way, they don't know if it is, they see it as any other little cars that are useless. They want a pickup so you can carry goats, you can carry lots of things. So I may leave home very disappointed, they didn't admire my car. In fact they think in terms of business that this car won't be useful. With a truck you can carry, when you want to go to the other village where there are uncles, you can carry all of us, but this one carries only three or four people.

MC: So would your songs reflect some of that kind of thing too?

AN: Well, perhaps in future. For now I was concentrating on issues to do with day-to-day life, especially bread and butter issues. It was interesting that yesterday, in fact the last of last week, people from Zanu PF were phoning me from the government side, not the opposition, saying, "You see there's a Congress, a Zanu PF Congress. You're wanted to do some poetry." I thought "What? I don't perform for a political party because I'll become partisan. They said, "Oh no, you're wanted by the big ones" (government leaders). So yesterday they followed up and I spoke to them, and I told them, "Look, I'll be away in Botswana, but you can get my group to come and do dances and so on and so forth, but I will not be around. But I was lying because I don't want to belong to a political party, because I'll not be neutral, I'll be very partial. So I want to criticize, whether it's a ruling party or a non-ruling party, for as long as I see that their policies are not good for the country. So I refused. I had to find a polite way of refusing. I am out of the town. But my group can come and perform.

MC: Very clever. So it looks to me like you're much happier doing your music for the next five years, or whatever. You're going to be doing your music and poetry.

AN: Yes, yes, yes! Actually I like it more at home. I do travel once in awhile, but I like it at home, because I do these things mainly for people at home. Whoever sees me fit to go to England or wherever, fine, I can do so. But I want to change things at home, I want to talk about the constitution indirectly, I will not be direct. I have to find indirect ways of saying, "But you guys are corrupt. How can you run a country when you find your nieces and nephews are being managers everywhere. You find a company, especially the public servants, you can't afford to employ your relatives and you are supposed to be the chief person, or the chief executive, or the director, right? Or when your uncle dies, or your father dies, your whole pool of employees has to go home, according to tradition and who is working then? You have to close the company or the department for two weeks for a week of mourning. So I talk about those things, and I've been a bit fearless. I say what I want, for which I have problems once in awhile. I've said, I'm not a politician, I leave politics to the politicians, but I, in any way I can will fight for the rights of my people, for the rights of citizens.

So if that is politics, then I'm a politician, but I'm fighting unconscious of the political element, saying things like, it is corrupt to take your uneducated niece to run your own bottle store, if you have one, your own business, because you're removing beer from there without paying for it. You talk of indigenization, perhaps a good idea, but what has been happening—I read a lot—newspapers, magazines, and you find always happening corruption, corruption, corruption. We are saying some of these people must be jailed, and they are not being jailed. What I was trusting this country for, is the judicial, that's what still remains, but sometimes there's a lot of interference. You find someone who's a murderer with all the evidence and they're acquitted, and you wonder, you begin to wonder if the judiciary is also becoming corrupted. Those are some of the things that one finds oneself looking at in terms of works.

MC: Yea. That's very interesting, I'm glad you mentioned all of that. Coming around to the music more, and the poetry itself, when you're on stage, or even when you're planning what you're going to do on stage, say, your next performance in Bulawayo, how does that work? I'm really interested in improvisation. What about you? How much do you improvise? Spontaneous things?

AN: Quite, plenty, quite a lot. I improvise quite a lot, in fact when the late VP passed away, Josh Nkomo, I was phoned by ZBC (Zimbabwe Broadcasting Company) to do something, because he was Ndebele and they didn't have enough stuff from the Ndebele. They asked me if I could do something, you know? I said, "What?!" The same day he died in the morning and they phoned me around 12 noon. I thought, "What can I do?" He said, "You know you are creative; do something." So I wrote this piece spontaneously almost. But memorizing is difficult for me, very, very difficult. Of course I'm busy with many other little things. So I produced something that even the newspapers and people still ask themselves, "Did you do that the same day? How come? Did you actually get it prearranged?" How did I know he was going to die?

So they asked me a lot, and then during the burial at Heroes Acres, President Mugabe said, "Thank you very much for a job well done." I think that he was surprised at the way in which I did it. I improvise quite a lot, both on stage, and sometimes even when recording. I remember once one poem that I did not have at all, and when we went for recording, I didn't know what I was going to put in there, and I did it at the studio. It's difficult, it's not easy. But I had to do it. But you see, my problem with improvisation in some of these songs that are known by the public is, that they end up knowing these from the recordings. They have copies, the latest. There's guitars, trumpets, drums, it's not like just mbira and poetry, it's modern stuff. And there's the singing. What happens is that I know where to come in and use mainly drum rolls to get me in. I communicate very much with the guy on the drums, and as I perform I know where the girls are coming in on stage and I improvise a lot. But some poems are now very well known by the public and sometimes they say, "Ah, you didn't do it right," especially children.

At some point, in Mutare, in 1996, I performed at the place called the Kwasa Kwasa from Zaire, based in France. So at the show, you're up there and the whole place is full and you're performing and you're having joy. Now you're finished, now I got drunk. I don't usually do so, but I had lots of frustrations. I was driving and I didn't have a good car. It was a kombie, a small minibus, and the front wheel burst at the side. I was driving and I controlled it, we stopped, we put the spare on and so on and so forth. I was late and tired and I was expected to be on stage. I didn't take long but before I went on stage I was drinking. So anyway, when I went on stage I was a bit off balance. I don't usually drink going on stage, but I forgot the poem that is well known in the country. And once you forget a line you've forgotten it all. The people said, "Get out. No, he's not the one, they sent someone else!" And I left. It was the last song apparently, and I pretended to be asleep in the car, because I knew my band members were going to be very mad at me! So there are things you cannot improvise! But there are lots of them you can improvise, so I do both. I improvise especially with those poems I know they don't know well. Usually radio popularizes one song, and the rest of the songs are left—people wondering—have you recorded this stuff? In fact it's five years old. So, with the ones that have been overplayed on the air, you can't afford to make a mistake.

So what you normally do is, I can go for about 30 minutes on stage and that's for a very quasi, very intimate audience, without a microphone. But if there is a microphone, 200-300 people, even 500, you do your performance, as long as there is the kind of microphone that you don't touch. People can hear, but they have to see you. It's unlike music where you are dancing out there, but with this one, they have to see you, your action. It's poetry, it's storytelling. However, with music, I can go for 30 minutes, but with music we play more. That's what we got used to most of the time. We start about 9 or 10 p.m. and finish close to 3, 4 and 5 a.m.

MC: People are dancing?

AN: Yea, and saying, "More. You can't even leave this day. I played in Victoria Falls. It was very difficult for me. They didn't want us to stop. And yet the contract said from 10 a.m. to 10 p.m. with many other activities, of course. It was a promotion by the ZRP, for their boarding school. No, we couldn't stop at 10 p.m., no. It was wild. Police had to do a lot of work to get the stadium under control. So we had to finish around 1 a.m., and still they didn't want us to stop.

What is happening is that there is a tendency to be selfish among us musicians and dancers. But with me, I decided to turn around and say, "Look, I will be old one day and this tradition must be carried on, music, poetry, dance. And I decided to establish the training program where students can go. I want you to go there and listen to that boy, that little boy who is there, and tell me if you want to promote that issue and listening to it, that's why I'm doing that. And for performances, I think my works are very good from what I've heard from people, and from what I have seen, with my own eyes, wherever I perform. Sometimes I see people shedding tears, like especially in Hawaii. The black folks especially, with comments like, "How do you do that?" Sometimes it 's emotional because I'm emotional, but I try and keep it balanced.

MC: But it's good to have *some* emotion.

AN: *Some*, yes!

MC: Now if we came to hear you in Bulawayo would it be in English? Would we understand what you're talking about?

AN: I fuse, I mix languages. I tell my stories in Ndebele and English, mainly, with a bit of Shona, but mainly Ndebele and English.

(I asked Albert about what instruments his group used)

AN: He said mainly drums, but someone faxed me from England saying, "It would be interesting to get you down." I'll be going down next year for four months. To Western Europe and England, mainly England. And he faxed me saying, "It would be nice to have mbira and drums recorded, and I said, "Well, it's worth trying."

MC: So you haven't really done that?

AN: I did it with Ephat Mujuru, live.

MC: But you don't have a recording?

AN: No, I think I'll do a recording in Europe. Perhaps in America, in Zimbabwe. I have something called Imboni (a group). It's instruments, and we have the ladies, five of them, and they perform mainly acappella, not like Ladysmith Mombasa. This would be ladies doing that, and there are five of them, and the sixth performer, I come at the end. They do most of the work. They sing and dance, but the style is more like Mombasa, a Zimbabwean version. So that's the one that really works while travelling. Six people is easier when travelling. And you can do it anywhere. But with me alone, you have to be sure that everything is ok (sound check, etc.) but with this one (Imboni), like when we were in Hawaii, we could stand on any street and start, because we didn't have these performance requirements.

So for me it was quite exciting, and they started saying, "You should come here, because, you don't need any instruments, just yourself and your voice and your traditional attire and being on stage."

CHIWONISO MARAIRE

Chiwoniso Maraire's family and musical background enabled her to have experiences unknown to the other musicians I interviewed. She truly represents mixing of traditional Zimbabwean music and Western popular music in what she does. She is a "culture-bearer" in the sense that she has brought traditional Zimbabwean music, handed down from her parents, to the West, as her father did. My fieldwork in interviewing Chiwoniso was uniquely informed by my knowledge of and friendship with her father, Dumisani Maraire, with whom I studied mbira in Seattle, Washington. Since I did not interview Dumi, and he died while I was in Zimbabwe, I felt fortunate to be able to talk with his daughter. The history of Zimbabwean music certainly includes Dumi's contributions for several reasons, one of which is his key role in bringing Zimbabwean music to the Western U. S., Canada and elsewhere. I wonder what Chiwoniso's role will be in preserving the musical legacy of her father? Will it be up to ethnomusicologists, Zimbabweans and others, to make sure this music is preserved in appropriate archives? Will the University of Zimbabwe library, in its music section, include this material in its permanent collection? I would hope so. What will be the role of the National Archives in Zimbabwe for recognizing Dumi's contribution?

Chiwoniso had an advantage over many Zimbabwean musicians in that her parents involved her in the recording process when she was very young. She learned about the recording business network, and the quality of performances required to produce high quality CD's. She also learned at an early age, from recording with her parents, important lessons about audiences and marketing, two crucial areas for successful performers. Chiwoniso understood that it was important for her to be a role model for women and especially women musicians. Although Stella Chiweshe and Beauler Dyoko are important in women's issues related to music, Chiwoniso and Busi Ncube represent younger Zimbabwean women musicians' concerns, and so have considerable influence upon the current musical scene as it affects women in music.

What does Chiwoniso bring to music in Zimbabwe that is special? She brings her diverse background and a strong sense of how to collaborate with various musicians to create something new and different.

Myrna Capp: Let's start at the beginning, if you would?

Chiwoniso Maraire: I was born in Olympia, in Washington State on March 5th, 1976, the oldest of the five children my mother and father had. My father, Dumisani Abraham Maraire, who was Zimbabwean by birth and of Zimbabwean/South African parentage, first moved from what was then Rhodesia, to America in the early 1970's, to study as an Artist in Residence at Evergreen State College in Olympia. This was made possible through the vision and assistance of Father Robert Kauffman, an American missionary who was working in the United Methodist Church, the church to which my father's family belonged, and for which my father had already begun to compose music. My mother came to America some years later, after she and my father had married. A little after I was born my parents moved to Seattle, where I spent the first six or seven years of my life. My father, being both an academic student and a very serious musician, began building a strong musical community in Seattle. He began teaching marimba and mbira lessons in the basement of our house. My parents were performing as well. A lot of the performances were in community halls and places where you could take your kids, so my siblings and I were there all the time. There would be someone watching/baby-sitting us during the hour or two our parents were on stage. My mother was a strong woman physically until later in her life. In the early years she was strong. I was once told that while she was pregnant with me, she performed until about two weeks before my birth. So from the time that I was me...was conceived...I was surrounded by music. My father told me sometimes my mother would take me as a toddler to the performances, wrap me up in something warm, lay me in my sleeping-basket, slide me under the bench for the bass marimba, and I'd sleep there.

So...my young life was about music and people. There were many people around, a lot of love within the family. In our home, we listened to plenty of music by other artists as well. This was the time of deep soul in American music, the late '70's. There was a lot of James Brown playin' in our house. My parents were crazy about him. They took me to my first James Brown concert when I was about two years old. I found pictures in my father's old stuff from that performance. Me, my father and James Brown. Amazing. There was a lot of Aretha Franklin goin on in our house. A lot of Rolling Stones and the Beatles, Roberta Flack, Taj Mahal, Gladys Knight & The Pips, Stevie Wonder, Marvin Gaye and Jimi Hendrix. There was a lot of music from serious

African musicians as well. Hugh Masekela was a favourite; he was also great friends with my parents and would visit whenever he was in the Northwest Coast area. My father listened to plenty of classical music as well, partly for school's sake, because he was studying music, but also because of a natural love for it. So there were a lot of different flavors going on musically in our house when I was young.

As far as our being raised in this house, as far as our whole relationship (for my siblings and I) was, concerning the instruments, marimba and mbira, our father was teaching in the basement. Our parents decided from early on that they weren't going to limit our relationship to and with these instruments. Basically, we could do as we wanted, how we wanted. My brother Ziyanai used to break marimba sticks all the time. He's a great marimba player now, but that was just his way, to drum the sticks on the floor until they'd break. He did that for a couple years. He used to bend all the spoons in the house as well, pretending to play marimba on the kitchen and living room floors. We gave him a nick-name because of that.

When I was about seven-and-a-half years old my family moved to Harare in Zimbabwe, where I was first enrolled in Courtney Selous Primary School in Mandara, then at Lewisam School (primary) in Chisipiti. I was in the school choir at Lewisam and I remember my father wrote a song for the school. The song was called, "We Are Children Of Zimbabwe" and I got to play drums in this song. It's important for me to mention the Lewisam School choir because the woman that led the choir is basically the person who taught me many of the technical aspects of singing I still use to this day. During the years that I was in the Lewisam School choir, I grew from being 'one of the gang' in the choir, to soloist, along with a friend of mine, Erin Spicer. Our voices blended well together. This woman's name, the choir leader, was Dee Wright. I always mention her, because it was incredible how she could handle children. It was incredible how she handled me. Although it was formal, the way that she taught the children, it was still just dealing with the kids. She would say, "Sing through your head. If you can't feel your voice coming through the top of your head, you're not singing." Little things like that. There you are, in the third grade, trying to feel your voice through your head (she laughs). Really? She was great. I did that for a couple of years. She also taught me the importance of using your diaphragm in singing.

Babam'kuru Nkosana, my father's older brother, passed away in the year that I turned nine. He and my father had been very close throughout their lives. My uncle was into educating the mind; he'd been a strong driving force behind my father taking the decision to come to America to study. They lived in the same house at one point in the early years in America. Babam'kuru Nkosana was also in America studying and they sometimes made music together. Being so close, my father was deeply affected by this death. My father wrote some songs about this and they became the foundation for the album "Tichazomuona." "Tichazomuona" was the first time that I sang on something that was recorded. It was the first time that I went to a studio and had an experience with recording machines. It was a great first experience because I had my parents there with me, so it wasn't too scary. I wasn't thrown into this by myself. And on that album I led two songs, with my parents singing the backing vocals. They did the rest of the songs together. This album was a big hit in Zimbabwe. People loved it. They used to play it all the time. Everywhere they played it. I was a little girl, nine years old. It's crazy when I listen to it now. I can't believe my parents let me do that! Squeaky little nine-year-old voice. It doesn't sound good, it's squeaky! But I was very close to my uncle as well, so I was deeply affected, at that young age, when he died. It was difficult. I remember I was really upset, because the guy who did the album cover misspelled my name. It was fixed later, but on the first batch of albums my name was wrong. I was very upset about that, I was so mad! "Dumi, Mai Chi and Chiwawiniso...Chiwawiniso! We all thought, that's not right!

By the time I turned eleven we'd moved back to the states. My father was in the University of Washington in Seattle again, this time studying for his Ph.D. My siblings and I were taking a very active role in the music. Our father built a powerful marimba band, Dumi & Minanzi III, in Seattle where we lived, and he was also performing on mbira. By this time my parents had divorced. They had been a musical team and had performed together for many years, but now, because of this situation it was no longer possible for them to do this. My father decided to put together a mbira group consisting of himself, my sister Tawona, my brother Ziyanai and myself. He named the group "Mhuri ya Maraire." Ziyanai did most of the hosho playing and backup singing. Tawona played the drums (traditional conga) and also sang backup, and I sang both lead and backup and played mbira with my father.

By this time I had spent some years playing and practicing on my own mbira which my father had given me while we were still living in Zimbabwe. The method in which my siblings and I learnt the instruments we played was very informal. Our father hardly ever sat us down for the specific purpose of teaching us how to play. Most times he'd say to us, "I want you to sing this, I want you to sing that" and from there we'd wing it and have a good time, but always with great focus. It was really a sort of free situation. We did rehearse though, with our father allowing us to create things along the way as we felt it in the music. At this same time my siblings and I were also rehearsing and playing in the marimba band, Mananzi III. The rehearsals for Mananzi III were a lot more intense as there were more people involved in the group. The members of the group were coming from extremely diverse backgrounds, all living in Seattle, all having previously been students of my father. Our father made sure that the rehearsals and performances my siblings and I were a part of didn't clash with our school responsibilities. As a result it wasn't possible for Ziyanai, Tawona and I to do many of the big trips with Minanzi III. I clearly remember when my father travelled with Minanzi III for performances and a recording session in New York, and how badly we wanted to go with the group, but it wasn't possible because we were in the middle of the school year.

In 1990 after my father completed his Ph.D. in Ethnomusicology at the UW he began preparing for us to leave the States and return to Zimbabwe. Mhuri ya Maraire had a farewell performance, our last performance, in Meany Hall at the University of Washington. The performance was recorded and released as a tape called "Imwe Baba." A few months after, my siblings and I left America with my father. My mother remained in the States.

My return to Zimbabwe with my family is when things began to get very interesting for me musically. I had expected that I was going to come and there was going to be people playing mbira all over the place in Zimbabwe. The community that I'd evolved in, in Seattle, our community, the people that surrounded me because of the music, were all musical people. Their kids played music, they played music; that's what our lives were about. There were community halls, there were festivals—musically life was rich. So we came over here to Zimbabwe and life was still great, but this musical thing wasn't happening. That was very frustrating for me. First, all the mbira players that I knew were older and almost all of them were men. I didn't know any young mbira players. I only met Ephat Mujuru's kids later; at that time I only heard that he had sons that played. I knew no girl of my age that played mbira. I still haven't come into contact with a girl of my age in Zimbabwe who played mbira since childhood.

I didn't know anybody who was playing, and that was very hard. There was no more marimba group. My father later put together a marimba group at the University of Zimbabwe and at the Zimbabwe College of Music, but it was very frustrating for him too, because

there weren't enough people that were playing. We went through this whole change, as a family. I was at school in Mutare and I was a part of the choir, and sometimes conducting the school choir, but now, musically, there was nothing going on compared

to what was happening in Seattle. A couple of months after we'd been here, I think I was about 15 or 16 at the time, I had come over to visit the family here in Harare. As I said, I was going to school in Mutare, with Tete Joyce, my father's older sister. I was in Harare during a school holiday, and one afternoon Ziyanai and I went to town. He was showing me Harare, and what was going on. We got to this place called Creamy Inn, it was the 'in" place where all the high-school kids used to go and buy ice cream and play video games. There were these two guys there, and there was an impromptu rap battle going on. There was this huge group of teenagers all trying to outdo each other. All the guys and the girls were cheering them on, trying to out-do each other in the lookin good thing. My brother happened to know half the guys that were there. He walks up to this group and he says, "Oh, my sister can rap better than all you guys put together and she can beat-box too." And I'm like, "Ziyanai, you didn't have to say that!" So these guys said, "You're not talkin about a girl rapping better than us! This is Zimbabwe, you know what I mean? No, no, no, no...A Zimbabwean girl? You've got to be joking." So then I thought, show them what you can do girl! So I did. I got up and did my thing.

So these guys were impressed. I was pretty happy with myself that day! The two guys I'd noticed earlier, Herbert Schwanborne and Tony Chihota were really good and they had their rap thing really going on, the two of them. They called themselves "Piece of Ebony."

Ziyanai introduced us (they were at the same high school), we started talking, and that's how I joined "Piece of Ebony." A lifelong friendship was formed that afternoon, and also the first rap group in this country that actually gained any sort of fame within the country, and in South Africa. We were mixing Shona and English lyrically, listening to a lot of the rap that was coming out of America, but not trying to copy the American style. We mixed a lot of mbira into the tracks we were composing to ride over. We weren't trying to copy anyone. This was one of the reasons why "A Peace of Ebony" worked, it was very original. Herbert, Tony and I were very similar in the sense that each of us were coming from mixed backgrounds. Herbert's mix was German-Zimbabwean, Tony's was Zimbabwean-Russian, and mine was Zimbabwean-American. We understood that we were different, but celebrated our Zimbabwean roots.

"A Peace of Ebony" was for me a great experience. I associated deeply with rap because of my many years living in America, but my musical performance life up until then had been centered solely on marimba, mbira and singing. All of a sudden I now had the chance to explore other sides of me—different styles of singing. Venturing into expressing myself through rap was extremely daunting at first. I've always been really into rap but I'd never tried to rap. To know that I could do that, that I could try, was liberating, and I was in a really great environment because the guys were wonderful. There was never any power trip thing going on. If anything, they were very protective, they were like my brothers. Like, "Don't mess with our sister" type thing. So that was great. In a very short space of time "A Peace of Ebony" grew. We were moulding our sound, building our image. We began spending a lot of time in Keith Farquhuarson's studio in Mount Pleasant in Harare. Keith is a white Zimbabwean of Scottish descent who had been working intensely in the black Zimbabwean music circle as a musician and producer for many years. He was one of very, very few white Zimbabweans to involve himself internally. He saw the huge potential in "A Peace of Ebony."

The result of our sessions in Keith's studio was the CD, "From the Native Tongue." Our following within the Zimbabwean urban youth intensified. Through Keith we were offered a distribution deal with a company in South Africa. They came over, we shot a video, and the video was great. It used to come out on TV here and in South Africa all the time. Our music was playing on the radio, but it wasn't available in the stores here because this was a South African company and they were more worried about making sure the stock was selling in South Africa. They weren't worried about Zimbabwe. I was still in school at that time. Then Herbert and Tony decided to move to South Africa. I couldn't move because I was in Form Four. That is a really important time in your education in Zimbabwe, and I didn't want to move anyway. I went down to South Africa once when we had a big interview for "A Peace of Ebony" and our CD, "From the Native Tongue." But that South African deal, it was a 'dud.' I never saw a cent of royalties. I still don't know what happened with that situation.

This is when things sort of started crumbling between the guys and Keith. We were so spread out, what with Herbert and Tony in South Africa. There was a lot of distrust that was coming into the whole thing, especially concerning how Keith had gotten the distribution deal. I remember Herbert and Tony just started feeling like we were getting ripped off, and I could totally understand that, because

they were seeing the situation first-hand in South Africa. I couldn't, I didn't know what was happening.

In 1994 we heard through Alliance Francaise in Harare about a competition called 'Les Decouvertes' hosted by Radio France International, and we decided to enter. Basically what it was, if you were a musical group from Africa or from any of the surrounding Francophone islands, and you weren't signed to anyone, whether or not you'd recorded before, then you could enter this competition. Basically it was a discoveries thing. Whichever band came out best would be awarded a lump sum of money to have a good time with, and also a recording and distribution contract. RFI can help you find contracts all over the world. So we composed a rap song that opened with a French refrain that Herbert's girlfriend, Karen Stally, sang, and we entered the song into this competition. We came first out of Southern Africa. "A Peace of Ebony" was flown to Madagascar for the finals and we came in third in the whole thing. This was a serious accomplishment because we were the youngest group by far, and there were a lot of groups taking part. So that was really great and made us feel really good as a group. Plus, all of a sudden we had all this money.

By now "A Peace of Ebony" had been together for about two years. We'd done a lot of things and I think we were just ready to do different things. Herbert wanted to go back and live in South Africa. He's incredible with video cameras, technical things, editing. He can make anything work. He's gifted in this way. So he wanted to go and work for a TV station down there. They'd offered him a job, and he was going to get well paid, plus gain a lot of experience. Tony wanted to travel, he wanted to have a good time. He'd always been that way. It was hard to get him anywhere on time, he just wanted to have a good time.

There were two new members in the group, George Phiri and Tendai Viki. George was an incredible visual artist and he still wanted to go and study that. Tendai was the serious brain of the group—he wanted to study medicine. I wanted to be in a different situation musically. I didn't want to stay in a situation where I was the singing girl in the rap band for the next five years, and I knew that. I wanted to do more things. I wanted to expand some more. So it just sort of came about at that time that people wanted to go in different directions. So what we did was, we split the pot of gold and everybody went to find their rainbow after that.

And this is the time that Andy Brown and the "Storm" started coming into play. What happened was, they—George and Tony, and Herbert, knew Andy from South Africa, because he'd been living in

South Africa at the same time. He'd recorded an album called "Gongonaland" when the guys were in South Africa, and they did some of the rapping on the album, because Andy's somebody who likes to make all these different styles. Andy, George and Tony, especially used to keep in touch. Keith had worked before with Andy for a long time as well, in a group called 'Ilanga,' that was incredibly successful in Zimbabwe in the 1980's."

Andy came from South Africa to record a new album called "Let Children Play." He was recording it in Keith's studio and he needed somebody to come and do some backup vocals. One of the girls that was supposed to do it had quit at the last minute and they were stuck. So Keith calls me one day and says, "Look, there's this guy that you really have to meet, and he needs somebody to do some backup work for him, and we've only got three or four days to finish the project, and you're the only person I know that can do it that quick. So I said ok, because, even though "A Peace of Ebony" had broken down, I was still going to Keith's studio a lot to do jingles. I used to make some extra cash that way in commercials and stuff like that. So there was connection still. So I said, "Ok, fine, you guys want this done last minute—I'm going to charge you guys a certain amount of money," which at that time was quite a bit of money, but it was fair considering the amount of work I had to do in such a short space. So Keith said "Ok, sounds pretty fair." He goes back to Andy and says, she is going to do it but she needs this much money. Andy says, "I'm not paying a singer that I don't know that much. Who is this person? I'm not paying that much money!"

We hadn't known each other at all. So Keith said, "She can do the job." Andy said, "I'm not paying that much money for somebody I don't know. I've never heard her sing." So Keith comes back and Keith made a mistake, because he told me straight. He says, "I talked to this man and he's not going to pay you this money," and I said, "I'm not singing on this album for this person. Who is he anyway? I don't know who he is, it's no big deal to me." So Keith says, "You know what, you guys have to meet. I will pay you the money and you go and you do the album." I said, "I will only do it because you've asked me to." Because by that time I was a little fed up with this man, Andy Brown, whom I didn't know, who assumed I wasn't worth paying. The ego of the artist! As far as I was concerned, he didn't want me doing it anyway.

I walk into the studio, this was the first day. There was a lot of tension and it was funny, because the other girl that was singing on the other album, Mwendi Chibindi, was also there. We'd been friends for awhile so it was cool she was around. We said, "Hey, hey, how you doin?" I walk into the studio and I start singing, I'm listening to this music, I'm thinking, "This is incredible music," but of course I'm not going to admit that (laughs). No, I'm saying nothing. We go in there in the booth, sing the music and oh man, this guy is really good. It shouldn't have been good, you know, I didn't want it to be, and I'm loving the music. We laugh about this all the time now, but he tells me that he was sitting in the studio that afternoon and thinking, "This girl can sing!" So that afternoon, at first, we're not talking to each other. But as the day wore on, the tension started to thaw and then there was a lot of laughter and jokes, just sort of finding out about each other's lives, and underneath it all we found a very strong bond.

MC: And it wasn't just music.

CM: No, it wasn't. There was a very strong connection, a similar understanding and appreciation for a lot of the same things. We finished doing the album and he went back to South Africa. A couple of months later I was at a café in town with a few close friends of mine and we were just talking about people that we'd met in our lives that had had a really great impact on each of us. I was telling them the whole story about how I'd wound up in Keith's studio recording with and for Andy, and as we were talking, Andy walked in the door! I was floored. I said, "Oh, hey when did you get back from South Africa?" He said, "Oh, I just got back today. I asked, "What are you doing here?" He answered, "Keith said I could find you here." I said, "What's the story?" He said, "I want to start a band, do you want to be part of it?" I said, "Definitely, I don't have to think about that."

Herbert was also around, for a few months. He and Andy had this idea of combining "A Peace of Ebony" with "Andy Brown & the Storm," which was a cool idea, but didn't work out. I started singing full-time in the "Storm." This was late '94. And again, it's amazing how things happen. Sometimes when you look back you realize that everything is sort of leading towards something, and it was now the next step for me.

I was in this situation, because, in "A Piece of Ebony," besides Keith and his studio and his keyboards, I was the only group member that played a musical instrument. The guys were rappers, so almost everything that we were doing was digital, playing with samples. Our stage performances were to DAT and we'd fill with choreography. Now I was in a live band situation and it was great, it was incredible! There's all the guys playing guitars and drums and keyboards and all these things were going on. I loved the experience, I mean I loved the "Storm." This was a different type of love to how I felt about "A Peace of Ebony." There were people within the "Storm" whom I was working with at that time, who, we were on the same level spiritually. Musically the "Storm" was made up of some of Zimbabwe's exceptionally gifted musicians; we were without a doubt the best band in the country for the four years we were together. Rehearsals were a serious affair. Mwendi, the girl I was in studio with for Andy's session, was in the "Storm" as well and together we redefined the role of the back-up singer in Zimbabwean pop music.

Although "A Peace of Ebony" had broken up, the record companies that had come to Madagascar when we went for the Les Decouvertes competition were still interested in something being recorded. And one of the French record companies, LusAfrica Sari, that had been in Madagascar, started trying to get in touch with me. They finally did, and they said, "We want you to do an album anyway. If you guys can't do it as "A Peace of Ebony" would you be interested in doing it as a solo musician?" Before making any kind of decision I ran LusAfrica's proposition by Herbert, George and Tony, because in all fairness we had originally been granted this opportunity as a group. They were completely behind me all the way, but I remember George's serious concern that I might be walking into a deal that wasn't as 'straight' as it appeared. In the "Storm" my music was starting to come out. Andy has always had a tendency to want to showcase the artists he works with in his group, if they are creating something. It's always been like that within the band, we're good with each other that way. So he said, "Who's next? Chi, bring your stuff." So by the time LusAfrica approached me, I was already performing some of my music on stage with "The Storm." Honestly speaking, I still felt like I didn't have enough experience. I was very wary about recording my first album. I was thinking, I'm not sure I'm ready to do this; I'm not sure that I'm able to do this. This was in '95 and I was about 19 at the time, so I was afraid to commit myself to something like that, but there was a lot of support coming in from Andy, from Keith and from my father.

They said, "You can do this. What are you talking about?" Another thing that concerned me was realizing the fact that the musicians who played serious mbira in Zimbabwe sang only in Shona. A lot my compositions that I wrote were a mixture of Shona and English textually, on a strong mbira base, then guitars, keys, brass, drums. In truth I saw myself as an English speaker of American birth who is heavily fluent in my mother tongue, Shona. I was unsure. Are people going to accept this? Maybe if I was in the States, you know, you could get

by with it and people would understand it, but I don't know if people are going to accept this in Zimbabwe. I was very much afraid of that, and again the guys were like, listen this is how you have been given your gift so use it as it is. Don't worry about what people are going to think. If you weren't supposed to do it that way you wouldn't have that kind of understanding of the instruments and languages.

MC: And they were right.

CM: Yea. I mean, hey, they were!

MC: Is this all leading up to "Ancient Voices" (CD)?

CM: Yea. So we got into studio and we started working. To send a demo tape to a record company you've got to put three tracks on it and then they listen to that to have an idea of what you're doing with it—if it fits in with their image and their company. So Keith and Andy, Adam Chisvo and I laid down three tracks and sent the demo to LusAfrica in France.

They loved it, and they sent a contract proposal straight away. So we took the normal six months or so to haggle about the contract, hone it down a bit, so that things weren't too one-sided on the side of the record company. At this time great changes were taking place within me also. I was pregnant with Andy and my first child, my daughter Chengeto. I would only have to start honoring the terms of the contract after her birth. Chengeto was born in 1996. In 1997 I began serious work on "Ancient Voices" with all of the other musicians in "The Storm" at Shed Studios in Harare. After we completed the recording and initial mixing, the master went to France with Keith where the final mix and production was done. "Ancient Voices" was released at the end of 1997.

There were many things I learned during that whole experience, firstly because these were the same members of "The Storm" but we were playing a totally different sound, a different style of music. It was great enlightenment for us to realize that we could do that, that we were open and versatile enough as musicians to be able to do that.

For me personally it was an incredible thing, because all of a sudden—it was scary at first actually—because I'm the type of person who, or I used to be—*I'm trying to get around that nowadays, because it's not always so good*—but I was the type of person at that time who didn't want to make people uncomfortable. I didn't like people to think I was stepping on their toes. I was always the girl who was trying to keep people happy, to keep the smile on your face, or do whatever it takes. And when you're in a situation where everyone's looking at you, you can't always be like that. There have got to be times when you've got to be like, "I want it like this. You may be thinking a different creative direction, but I am thinking this." I had to learn to do that, so that was a growth thing. I was used to other people doing that. My father was a man who was very strong in his ways. My husband, Andy, is a man who is very strong in his way. I had grown accustomed to being surrounded by men who take the initiative, and I'm in the background but with them, creating upon the base they have placed. So that was an important turning point for me. Because I was working with some of the greatest Zimbabwean musicians in the studio, the time that we spent together was really great, but it was also a personal challenge. All in all we had fun in studio, working hard. We would grab lots of food and a couple crates of beers. A good time. We used to sit in studio and have a good time. By the time you finish you're trying to find your way to the door. Is that the door? It was intense recording, but plenty of fun.

MC: Your Dad was kind of that way too. He had a good time?

CM: Yea, he was, he was like that. I mean it was never formal, my experience with music was never formal. It was always part of having a good time. But you're working, FOCUS, you know, and you know what work is, and you're doing that work and you're finishing it, but still, have a good time.

MC: That seems to be a special part of you, and obviously the people around you.

CM: Yea, we party, we party a lot, we have a good time. We fight a lot too as a result. The only formal sort of experience I had with music was at the Zimbabwe College of Music. I'm surprised I lasted there so long because I was going crazy, not because of the establishment itself, but just because my whole understanding and relationship with music was very personal, it was very much like breathing. I didn't think about it. I was graced enough to be bestowed with the ability to learn by ear. I'm very fast in that. Once it's there, it's there. I can remember songs from twenty years ago, when I was a kid, so it was really hard for me to be in a situation where you (did it differently). It was great to learn composition from an educational perspective and to learn how to write music as well, staff notation, it was great to learn that. But I hated the rigidity it set to the music sometimes. That for me was very difficult and still is even now.

For me, music is flow, you see? But I learnt to accept, through my father, that to study your gift, your talent, and understand the technical aspects of it, enhances your gift. I learned that it was great to have Chopin's music there in front of you and be able to READ it. You can still play it hundreds and hundreds of years later, but the thing for me was, can't you listen to that same music that he wrote and play it the way that you feel it? Why do you have to read the music exactly? I'm not saying ignore what the man did. He was one of the greatest composers ever. This is how Chopin felt it, you know what I mean?

But once in awhile I want to feel it differently . No, no, no, you don't do that, not in classical music. So that was sometimes very difficult for me to deal with. Still, it was important for me to experience this. It was important to learn staff notation. It was important to learn that there were other ways people heard music besides the way that you hear it, and to have to learn to appreciate that.

MC: You have a big advantage in that because a lot of the other musicians don't know these things. You know those things.

CM: I had to learn to be—it's ok if somebody sees it different than you. Just accept it. I used to get into fights with the teachers all the time. Like, don't do this to me, please, music's not supposed to be that way.

MC: Now what do they think about what's happened to you now?

CM: Ah, they're so supportive, everybody's supportive. A lot of people are saying, we're not surprised. The hard time you gave us, something had to happen. I didn't always make it very easy for some of the teachers, I remember. For example, because I'd been playing marimba for so many years, and mbira for so many years. It came naturally and it was really hard because two of the guys that were teaching marimba at the ZCM didn't like that I was so far ahead. Initially they tried constantly to 'put me in my place' as a student. I would get bored in class. I would rebel. There were some people there who could really play, then there were people there who had not had experience with marimba. Because you play something, you can see that that person knows what they're doing. What used to really upset me is, people were not grouped according to their abilities, they were just grouped, like your name was picked out of a hat and you're in that class. And I was like, this is not working, it's not fair to the people that can play, it's not fair to the people that cannot play. Frustrating! You're going to build a very bad situation. So we secretly rounded ourselves up with the people that were able to play and we started our own little group.

It was funny because in the early days before we'd finally sorted out the grouping situation, marimba class would start at 2:00 p.m., ending at 4, and at quarter to 3 I'd walk in the door. And the guy that teaches the class used to get so mad at me, and now he's one of my really good friends. But I couldn't sit through two hours of this. I'm just not that type of person, I couldn't do it. It hurt. I'd walk in there and he'd be teaching the class and he'd take a mark off or something like that. I knew every single time that he was going to do that and so what I'd do, I'd get in there and listen for a couple of minutes and then start playing. He hated that. I'd ask what we're doing and he would tell me and I would say, "Oh, that's where we are."

So there were some funny experiences at the Zimbabwe College of Music. We're really good friends with everybody there now. A couple of the younger teachers come to my performances all the time; one of them just gave me a copy of his new album. It's pretty good! But in the early days, ZCM days, we knew how to turn those screws on each other, man. He'd always get me back by being the teacher. I always thought I was better than teachers.

MC: Are there some things that you really want to have be a part of this interview that I haven't asked you about? One topic that I'd love to hear you talk about if you want to would be, when you write a song or when you're doing a song, when you improvise on it, when you play around with it, this whole thing of improvisation, how you do that, and how your group does that. Is it like in jazz? Do you take turns doing your solos or whatever? Is that something you want to say anything about?

CM: Yea. Definitely. We do take turns with each other and first of all for me, music is God, that's what it is. We as human beings come into it when it comes to producing the sound so that other people can hear it, but otherwise, as far as I'm concerned, music is an element of God, pure and simple. And a lot of the people that are in the band, or that were in the band before—we've got different people now who treat it in different ways—but the people that were in the "Storm," the first strain of the "Storm" that I was in, felt the same way about it. You'll find that in some groups there will be songs that you're doing and, from the technical point of view, someone would say, "Oh, you weren't supposed to put your solo there, because when we rehearsed it, in the rehearsal room you weren't playing the solo

there, so why are you playing a solo there now?" There was very little of that in the band and it still is hardly there now.

There are times when you're playing and you can feel something, and it's there, it's real. We've always had this understanding, play it before it goes, you know what I mean? Because if it's there you should just play it. You have to, you're actually doing the wrong thing if you don't play it, because you're supposed to play it. So if you aren't playing it, you're doing me an injustice, you're doing yourself an injustice, you're doing the God that gave you the talent an injustice if you don't play it, so play it! But, you have to have a serious understanding of and respect for music and the musicians you are performing with to be able to do this on stage at the right time, and not break the flow.

And this is, for me, composition. It is impossible for me to sit down and write a song—to wake up one day and say I'm going to write a song. It doesn't work that way for me. Songs come. It's like you wake up one day and something comes into your head (Chi hums) that's kind of cool. If I'm busy I put it down on a tape, if I even get around to it. Then, after that, it's the words, you know. same thing. I wait for the words to come and put that down.

When I get a paragraph I write it down. It's been very few times in my life that I've been lucky enough to be given a whole song at one time, words, music and all. Usually it comes in bits and pieces. If I get a paragraph and I sit there and I try to add to it, because that's the particular subject, it doesn't always work. I tend to write from the heart. I tend to write from experiences that I've been through, things that are close to me, things that I've seen. It's hard for me to just write, because this is what we're singing about, when I'm writing for myself.

On the other hand, when I'm writing and composing a score for film, I don't have this problem at all because I draw ideas from the script I'm working with and the unedited scenes I watch with the director. This was the case when I worked on Zimbabwean films such as, 'More Time' and 'Everyone's Child.' Both musical scores earned critical acclaim in Southern Africa and overseas. "Ancient Voices" CD, on the other hand, is a very personal album because every single song on that CD is something that I've either been through, or somebody's been through, and they told me about it, and because they are close to me I am able to relate deeply to this experience. Or it's something that I've seen, or maybe something that I've read about. But there was nothing there that I just penned down. So I'm not very technical when it comes to music and the whole composition thing. It's a very inside thing for me, it just comes out. Incidentally, "Ancient Voices" received the 'Best New African Artist' award from RFI in 1998.

MC: What about what's going to happen next for you, because you're probably in for another bit of a change here in your life with a new baby, and the sudden death of your father. Your Dad was kind of your mentor, but you're on your own now, and you seem strong.

CM: There's a much bigger picture. I'm starting to feel like time that's spent here—it doesn't make sense to me that you do all these things just to die. As in that death is the final stop, y'know? These things that I learned from the death of my mother, my brother, my father. Losing people that close in a very short space of time, at a young age, makes you stop and think. What am I supposed to be doing with my life? How am I supposed to be acting? What am I supposed to be learning? Music is a vehicle I ride deeper into the mysticism of life. Am I on my own? Perhaps we are all, a little, on our own. But I also have my two daughters, my siblings as well. So I'm not completely on my own (smile). Sometimes I hear the voice of my mother speak to me. The first time it happened I was unsettled by the experience. Now I welcome it. Subconsciously I know I search for the voice of my father, these days. There is far more beyond the existence we experience here, on this level, now. Of this I'm certain. Sometimes, I want to be a doctor. I remember when I was younger, whenever I was asked, "What do you want to be in life when you grow up?" I'd always answer "a pediatrician." Go figure! Who knows? Maybe...

AMAI (FRANCESCA) MUCHENA

Interviewing Amai Muchena was probably the most difficult, but rewarding, of all the interviews I conducted. Her English was very limited and I knew no Shona, so arranging the interview by phone was difficult. Amai's friend translated for us, but at times I felt unsure of what was being said. On the other hand, there were many reasons that this experience was a very special one! Going to Amai's home in a high-density suburb (township) in Harare was an eye-opener. It was a very small, simple, and austere house by Western standards. Having a traditional meal together--mealie meal and sauce eaten with our fingers—no silverware--was a challenge, but fun. And especially the MUSIC! The singing and dancing, so typical in Africa, the movements just flowing from the music, and playing mbiras and hoshos, was most enjoyable. It seemed like a festive party.

I was told ahead of time that Amai loves to make a dramatic "event" of such a situation and she certainly did. We loved it! Amai's passion for music permeated the interview. Use of music for Zimbabwe's independence, to educate about AIDS, to inspire and educate children musically, and to work to preserve traditional music were themes of her musical life which she addressed as we talked. She believed that the spirits called her to sing, dance, play mbira and hosho, and be possessed. Because of this she seemed close to traditional Shona ways.

Note: My daughter, Kristin, Claire Jones and I arrived at Amai's home in a "high density suburb" outside of Harare on the 5th of December, 1999, and were greeted with the following:

A small group of children chanted (in Shona, in rhythm, with ulalation), a welcome for us.

Amai Muchena: Welcome!

Vimbai, granddaughter of Amai Muchena, sang a chant-like song in Shona. Amai had taught Vimbai this song in a creche (preschool).

Myrna Capp: Thank you! (our group clapped and cheered)

Alice Kanali (TR, translator)), *a friend of Amai's and our translator for the interview:* They are saying (singing), "AIDS, AIDS the untreatable disease. This comes to the father, and then goes to the mother, and then comes to the child." That's what she was saying. "What wrong have I done to be in this situation, what wrong have I done to deserve this?" That's all what she was saying.

MC: Thank you.

TR: Thank you. (children leave the room)

MC: I want to talk to you about your life.

AM: All of my life?

MC: Yes. When you were born, where you were born, and that kind of thing.

AM: My name is Francesca. My mother's name is Veronica. In 1950 I was born, June 25th

TR/AM: Her father is Michakoko.

AM: Since 1950 I play some drums. I go to school myself. I did traditional dancing. I used to go there when I was very young to take water to give them that svikiro (spirit medium).

TR/AM: When she was a baby she would dance to any musical thing. If drums were being played, when they put her down, she would start dancing to the music. Also, there's a spiritual medium, which possesses her, Chipoko. When she was a small girl, she used to fetch water for the spiritual medium. She was a favorite. She used to go to the well and collect water and bring to the medium. In 1961, that's when she met her husband, Mondreck, a teacher of mbira. In 1965, she went to school and wasn't very much interested in school. When something happened she would just go back home, and this was being caused by the spirits. In 1964, during the liberation, that's when she started singing for the liberation struggle. She was a very good singer motivator for the people who were doing politics.

TR/AM: Her husband, Mondreck, never proposed love to her. There was a bira ceremony, where people gathered to play the mbiras. Then the mediums possess who ever they want to possess. Mondreck had a brother, Eric, who started playing mbira and they started singing. When Amai sang, Eric was possessed by the ancestral spirits and they said to him that this young lady is going to be married to his brother. Around this time, Amai's first son (who she had by a teacher, Darefinos), was four weeks old. When she gave birth to her child, for two weeks she was trying to breast feed, but then she took the baby to her mother who tried to give him milk. Her mother did her best, she used to look for milk and most of the other things that are needed by a child.

Amai was working in Mabelreign. There's a beerhall in Shearwood behind the bawa (bar) where she used to work. She used to do double work, in the bar, and then in the hall. As we have said before, the spirits said they wanted her to be a muroora, to be a daughter-in-law in their family. Before Amai and Mondreck got married, she was impregnated by Mondreck, so she had twins by him in 1965. When she gave birth to Trymore, her first child, she gave him to her mother (or grandmother), when he was only four weeks old. Then she married Mondreck. In '65 she fell pregnant again by Mondreck, and that very year she gave birth to twins, in 1966. The twins died between three and four years.

She says Mondreck had another wife before her, but then they divorced. Her father, Michapon, was against the affair, because, he was saying, why did Mondreck leave his other wife. He was scared that she might be left. In 1967 he paid lobola officially. The husband pays lobola—"roora" in Shona—to the wife's family. Lobola was twelve pounds in those days; it was a lot of money. It was seven kettles, but he never gave the kettles to the boss (father). Mondreck, with the ex wife, had other children, Jessica and Maximus. So Amai took those children to stay with them, and gave them the names of the deceased. So Jessica was given the name of the late Moyo (Paid-amoyo), and Maxmo was given the name of Madzudzo. And there was another child, Cosmas, the firstborn of Mondreck. They never changed the name, just named him Cosmas. (*they also took over the birth certificates!*)

MC: Amai, I have a question. You didn't mention music earlier in your life, I'd like to know, were you doing music when you were a child, was there music around you?

AM/TR: Oh yes, I talked about it, about the biras. I grew up to the music. They were practicing music every day, playing mbira. All my life.

MC: Even in your home?

AM: Yes.

MC: So your parents were doing music too?

AM: Yes, I grew up to the music.

MC: Then, when you were with Mondreck, that's when you started doing it more publicly, with him, for audiences?

AM: Because we were together we play mbira, for a long time. Myself, I sing, I dancing, I play hosho, drums. So I meet him, Mondreck, myself I was proficient in everything, altogether. So every day even, I put food here, after that Mondreck plays, and myself. I do it for practice. Every day.

MC: And the children are with you?

AM: Ah yes, dancing, very well. Publicly, I take a group of children like that. I was teaching creche (preschool). What I was doing was starting a business. A creche for her income/business.

MC: And will music be a part of the creche? Will you bring some music for children?

AM: Yea.

Claire Jones: When you saw Vimbai (Amai's granddaugher who sang when we arrived), what she did, she learned at creche.

AM: I was teaching her. Every thing she did I was teaching her.

MC: When you were with Mondreck and doing music, were you travelling around? You were a group, the two of you, and then some others too, were a group? ("Mhuri Yekwa Muchena")

TR: They used to travel all around Zimbabwe and Europe, Mozambique.

AM: I remember those days. They are a dream. (Claire and Amai talk about going to Mozambique). I come back, I go again, to Maputo (capital of Mozambique). Sometimes to Chimoyo, Tete.

MC: So mostly to Zimbabwe and Mozambique and then to Europe?

AM: Yea, Germany, Mondreck, not me.

CJ: Oh, yea, Mondreck, the other times.

AM: They are going again.

CJ: Yea, she was not always included in these trips, for example in 1990.

MC: And then, since that time, just to complete the chronology...but I like you telling about the music as you tell about your life. So let's do both if you can. Since you did those tours and traveled around, what have been your main activities, like right here near Harare with your family. Doing music locally mostly?

AM; Yes, there are so many people here in Zimbabwe.

TR/AM: She said they used to do performances with her husband, and when they sang, just the two of them, it was so great, without anybody interfering. One time in London she was doing actions on stage and the audience all rose up to cheer.

CJ: The two singing together. One can go and try to find the (tapes), but it's difficult, and the same thing with the old singles. Sometimes we go check in the National Archives, and I haven't done it.

MC: What will happen to the music now that Dumi is not alive? What will happen to things like that, that were in his possession? Is that going to be up to Chiwoniso, Dumi's daughter?. Or his family, or what? Do you know? What will happen to his tapes and things like that?

AM/TR: I think they will go to Chiwoniso (Dumi's daughter).

MC: Another reason I'm asking is that Dumi had presented a lot of tapes and some other things, to be promoted at the University of Zimbabwe to Senior Lecturer.

CJ: I was going to say, I'm sure the University of Zimbabwe may have interest in these. *(They are there at U.Z.)*

AM: I've got a book right over here. Dumi did a very good job. If I go to America, then I want to come back here and go to the University. I go in there, I sit down, I talk to Mr. Shekori and ask him if they like it. She mentions other names in Shona. They all like it.

CJ: When Dumi came here doing his research.

TR: After he left, when he was in America, he wrote to the University of Zimbabwe. He wanted to come and share research about the music, everything about the culture. He was so rejected, and then Dumi Maraire came to Mai Muchena and presented the problem to her, and then she went to Shekori and she presented the problems, and Shekori was very interested, saying, look, if it means preserving our culture, we better help. We had to make all the arrangements for Maraire.

AM and TR: Maraire came here.

CJ: We played together.

AM: So Dr. Maraire used to come with his wife, Mai Chi. She knows our culture. Mai Chi knew how to play the shakers, she used to play marimba as well, and dancing, and she used to play drums as well.

CJ: He only had one wife, Mai Chi, the one that died in 1997. He would have been with her five years ago. They were divorced in Portland. He had left Zimbabwe in 1986 and had been living in the States.

MC: When I was talking to Joyce Jenje Makwenda she said to get Amai talking about some of the other musicians who are on my list, because Amai has some interesting things to say about the musicians.

(I asked Amai to talk about musicians who she knew, as Joyce Makwenda suggested, including ones that Amai had inspired)

AM/TR: It is just natural, it just happened that she influenced other musicians. It is something that is inborn within her. She is one who has been helping others to go on top.

TR: She said that Stella Chiweshe used to come here, and Amai used to help her with the correction of five year olds, some of the music. She used to come and pick me up here and we'd go to her place and we'd help each other. And when Amai would go wrong, she'd say, "No, no, no, why don't you do it this way?" Yes, that was Stella Chiweshe!

CJ: A part of "Mother Earth." (an organization)

AM: Yes, I used to go there. Dumi Maraire also went to this organization, "Mother Earth." They said members should donate about $400. So when each person paid the $400, they were saying we should go and look for donors, and the donors could give them more money so they can do their projects, whatever they wanted to do. So when all this money came, Stella Chiweshe and others kept on asking.

AM/TR: What she wishes for most is to start a school to promote cultural things. She wants to teach children, or anybody else who is interested in culture, or a preschool, about African music. But the thing is, finance is the problem. Stella grew up being a poor person, but riches were in her mouth and her music. Financially, Stella wasn't very stable. *(Claire Jones gives money to her)*

(Traditional dance was mentioned)

TR/AM: Amai used to be a very good dancer.

AM: If I've got a funeral, I go, they play that music.

TR/AM: At a funeral, in their homes, they play Jerusarema; Amai says that they like "Jerusarema" (a traditional Zimbabwean dance). Each medium, each spirit, has his own song. If I have a spirit that possesses me, the spirit has got a very favorite song. Just sing that song, and the spirit comes and possesses me. So I've got another musical gift; it's a type of song.

AM: It's a Mozambican song and dance.

CJ: Can you maybe talk about the pottery?

AM: For every woman, the best room in the house is the kitchen, and her utensils. Each woman has got to have her own utensils. So every homestead, in the kitchen, there are the clay pots, and these clay pots also have a meaning. The ones on the top, those are for the ambuyas, the grandmothers; and the ones in the middle are for the great grandmothers; and then at the bottom we have the great, great, great, great grandmothers. By the pots, you must sit down. With these big ones at the bottom, for the great, great, grandmothers she can't just take them. She has to kneel in front of these pots and then tell the spirit, no, there's nothing inside there. My friend has come, has come to collect me to go and look for something. But when I come, they know I'll bring something to fill this pot for you. Yes, that's why she was kneeling down; and then you clap your hands, telling, ulalating as well (Amai ulalates).

CJ: So anytime there's something big happening, they'll be addressing the pots.

TR: For the grandmothers, they have their pots. If it's the grandfathers, they have their pots as well.

CJ: One for each.

TR/AM: Yea, your own cup, your plates, yes. These are your things. When you die you are buried with your favorite things.

(We all go outside to the veranda beside the house to play music, dance and listen.)

AM/TR: It's like this song, I wrote it for my mother who is "late" (deceased). I'm just lamenting. I wish my mother was still around because she is the one who used to help me with my problems. (Kids and TR sing together). This song is a dedication to my mother.

Note: What followed was a wonderful time of playing mbiras, hoshos, and dancing outside on the veranda, with children and adults participating. Kristin took many photographs, with family members asking for more and more photographs. It's unfortunate that I was not able to videotape this because the music and dancing could only be captured fully on video. Sadly, my video camera had been stolen in a theft in our rented home in Harare.

COSMAS MAGAYA

I had heard of Cosmas Magaya but had never met him until I attended the Zimbabwe Music Festival in Seaside, California in July, 2001. I heard him play mbira and attended a mbira workshop session which he taught. I also heard him explain about his involvement in the Nhimbe project, an aid, self-help program in Mhondoro, Zimbabwe, started by some people from Eugene, Oregon. I was told that Cosmas was the kind of person that I should consider including in my book project. Later, I learned that Cosmas' wife had died and he is raising their four children.

As I got to know him in the interview process, and in talking informally with him, I realized that he was a special person and a fine musician and teacher. Qualities that I saw in Cosmas, from my brief time talking with him were wisdom, caring, thoughtfulness, and diligence. He seemed to me to be trustworthy, and a very ethical person. He was systematic in his approach to assisting and helping his village in the Mhondoro area, working closely with a network of musician friends in Eugene, Oregon, who had taken on this project in part because they liked and respected Cosmas, a nice compliment!

At the Zimbabwe Music Festival in Seattle, 2002, I met and visited briefly with Cosmas' daughter, who is now a student at the University of Oregon in Eugene. Cosmas has wisely used the opportunities he has been given to better himself, his family and his village in Zimbabwe. He is a true leader, yet he is humble and unselfish. His friend and musical colleague, Beauler Dyoko relies on Cosmas to help her because her English is quite limited. He willingly gives her the help she needs, such as offering to read and make corrections in the interview I did with her, because she is not able to do it.

In his teaching of the mbira class, which I took from Cosmas in 2001, I observed that he was patient, explained things well, demonstrated as we needed it, and paced the learning appropriately. Fortunately for all of us, Cosmas left the business world and is making his living performing and teaching music. As an informant for Paul Berliner's book projects, Cosmas played an important role. The world of Zimbabwean music, locally and abroad, is enriched because of Cosmas' musical talents and warm personality.

Myrna Capp: Where are you from originally?

Cosmas Magaya: I'm from Mhondoro. I would say it is southwest of Harare when going toward Msvingo.

MC: When were you born?

CM: In 1953, on the 5th of October.

MC: Tell me a little bit about the early part of your life and especially the musical part of it, could you? Include something about your schooling in the early part of your life.

CM: When I was about eight years—that is when I actually started getting much involved in music. Of course, even before that, I used to hear a lot of music. My parents, they are Catholics; they were married in the Roman Catholic church, and also they are followers of that until today. But at the same time my father had a long history of what he went through because of the ancestral spirits, which were kind of haunting him, wanting to possess him. As a result of that, about four kids died before my elder sister, and I were born. But that had to be rectified by having a ritual ceremony, and then that spirit was appeased. Then my father started having some children. The type of spirit which wanted to possess him was a tribal spirit, which does not like one to be bedding (sleeping) with women, because it regards bedding (sleeping) with a woman as dirty before the formal traditional ritual.

So that was the reason behind that. But then my grandfather had to consult a specialist, a specialist who is a nyanga, who advised him to brew some beer and slaughter—in honor of that spirit—only one cow. "How can I do that he wondered," and then the specialist told him, "You are going to reap more things if you do that." So after he did that, then my father started dreaming about some herbs. And then he started being shown herbs, being in the forest, and then he started practicing as a herbalist. Coming back to the music, mbira players such as Bandambira and others were hired to perform at our village, before I even learned how to play mbira.

Then, coming back to how I started to play mbira myself, at the age of eight, I happened to be living with a cousin/brother, Ernest Chivanga. Ernest Chivanga was the son of my mother's eldest sister, and this Ernest came from Marondera area. The Marondera area is a place where a lot of mbira players used to be. There used to be a very big spirit in that area. So his brothers used to perform for that big spirit together with Bandambira. So my mother, because of the situation that—Ernest's father was a polygamist—he had about four or five wives, and my mother was not happy about that. She talked to her sister and asked her for permission for me to be with Ernest Chivanga. They agreed and Ernest came to stay with me. Then Ernest, since he was a mbira player, I started learning from him. So that's just briefly how I started learning mbira. Since I was so young Ernest did not want to teach me how to play mbira because he felt that I would put his mbira out of tune. So each time he played I would observe his fingering from a distance and when he was absent in the fields, I would sneak into his hut and begin putting into practice what I had seen him doing. Unfortunately one of the days he came back from the fields without my knowledge and as he approached his hut he heard some mbira being played inside and he stopped in the veranda of the hut for a few moments listening and then all of a sudden he showed up on the door. I was stunned, but Ernest said to me, "Do not worry, I have proved that you are very keen to learn how to play mbira and as from today I am going to teach you."

Ernest was surprised that I was able to play the song called Karigamombe just from observing him play from afar and that was my first song. But of course, I gained some reputation. When I was twelve—in the Mhondoro area—the group gained some reputation for mbira playing. We were now being hired, people coming from different parts of the region—coming to hire us. Then I went to St. Michaels school. It was a boarding school, a missionary school.

That is the school I attended, and, they didn't allow mbira playing during those days. They didn't allow that, so I had very difficult times when I moved from my primary school, going for my secondary education—going there. I experienced some problems. I was very much married to my instrument. But when I went there, they didn't allow me to play my mbira. So as a result of that, there is a teacher, I can't say his name, but he was very much interested. I think he had heard that I was an mbira player. He wanted me to teach him how to play mbira, but I was scared. I thought this was a trick and I could be expelled from school. So this teacher ended up begrudging me to the extent that sometimes I was being beaten up. Sometimes I was being sent to go for weeding in the fields—practical odd jobs. They said that if you did something wrong you are punished or penalized by being sent there to do that. So I used to be sent, until another time, one of my friends said, "Why don't you just show him something what you do; this will help your situation with him." Still I was scared, but I ended up agreeing to talk to him about my mbira life. I told him, "I played a little bit, a little bit of mbira." Then he said, "Can you show me?" Then I started showing him. Then he was very happy.

From that day our relations changed and he said, "From today you are no more going to be doing any odd jobs. You are going to be an assistant to the person who repairs some soccer/footballs as well as some shoes for the nuns and priests.

I wasn't playing music at school, but after schooling, each time during school holidays, I would go back home and perform, playing my mbiras. That was when again I started joining hands with Mr. Mude of Mhuri Yekwa Rwizi. Mr. Mudi who is the leader of the group. His mbira group was a well-known group for playing music which the ancestral spirits liked. Their playing style was so famous that we kept on being hired.

GC: We went to the Mujuru home for a bira, out by Rusape.

CM: They have a long history, the Mujurus. They are quite a big name, and also into music. At one stage we used to play together, myself and Ephat Mujuru. Yes, played together in the 60's, 1970's. He's such a good musician, Ephat. We used to play together for Mr. Mudi.

MC: So what was the next step, the next stage for you? Does that group still exist, or what happened next?

CM: You know, that group still exists. I had to move to Bulawayo because I really wanted to get a better job. After I obtained a diploma in marketing, I really wanted to get a job, but there was Olof Axelsson, who was at the College of Music—Kwanangoma. At that time he really wanted my music—the way I played mbira, so he wanted me to get a diploma in teaching at Kwanangoma. So I went to Kwanangoma and spent about three months. My elder cousin/brother—who still lives in Bulawayo, was not all that happy because at the College I would get some training—we were working, making some marimbas and mbiras, and I was teaching mbira to some students, but they were not paying me well during that time. It was $12 a month, so this cousin/brother of mine did not like that. So I started applying for a job. I got a job at the Dairy Marketing Board. They wanted a sales representative to do the high density area shops. I applied. There were so many applications, more than twenty, but then I was offered that job, because I had a drivers license and my diploma, so I was ready. So I got a job and I worked there. Each time I got my annual leave I would go to Mhondoro and continue playing mbira, but still, in Bulawayo, I established some playing. I started teaching some local people who were interested. I was playing mbira with David Maveto who was employed at Kwanogoma College. I was kept very busy, and of course during my life I also did some teaching. I met with Paul Berliner in 1971.

When he came to Zimbabwe, he went to the Broadcasting Corporation. He didn't know which group to get to, so he went to the Broadcasting Corporation and met somebody who was there, head of that African department—Dominic Mandizha. Then he said, "Can you please play me some mbira recordings for all the artists you recorded in Zimbabwe? So the recordings were played—all the artists—then he chose our group, our recordings of Mhuri Yekwa Rwizi. He said, "How can I meet with these people?" That was what Dominic Mandija said, "You wait until when I finish work and I will take you to the place where Mr. Mudi works at B and B Motors in the city." He did that, and then Paul was introduced to Mr. Mudi. Paul left in the evening, drove to Mr. Mhuri's house, and then he said, "Please, I want to learn mbira from you, can you teach me?" Then Mr. Mudi said, "Ok, I'm going to assign you to who is going to teach you." Then I and Luken were assigned to teach Paul Berliner, so that is how I came into contact with Paul Berliner.

MC: Have you seen his book about jazz improvisation?

CM: I haven't read it. I think it would take me some months.

MC: Me too. So how long did he study mbira with you?

CM: He studied mbira with me ever since he came to Zimbabwe in 1971.

MC: Do you have any more information you can tell me about your music, any other things that happened to you that are very interesting? Like maybe a particularly interesting performance, or even one of your most troubling performances, or something that was very difficult for you—a story you'd like to tell me about?

CM: When I was young, maybe around twelve years, when there was a performance at Bandambira's area, he was not there. People wanted to hire him to perform at that bira but they could not find him. So they heard that at Magaya's there were some good mbira players, so people traveled to our place. It was around 5 or 6:00 in the evening when they arrived. At that time I was suffering from chicken pox, so my body was full of measles itching. So my mother, upon hearing that, she didn't like it! But my father, he really liked it. So my father decided—"we'll just have to put him on a bicycle carrier—then he can go perform for them." My mother didn't like that, but since my father

liked it, and since I was going to be paid a little something, which was going towards supplementing my school fees, my father insisted.

I was put on the carrier and I went there and performed. But as you perform, you sweat, and so I had two distinct things which I wanted to accomplish. One was to—I tried to play well—but I also wanted to *scratch*! And the other something—I wanted to convince people that I can play well. So I kept on my mbira playing. That's why I can't forget that day. All the spirit mediums got possessed. One of the spirits said, "You shall see where this young man is going to end; this music is great, he shall be a great player." That was said when I was so young and I didn't believe it.

The thing which I wanted to pass on to the young players—I think maybe can be helpful, is, although I was very much interested in my mbira playing, there were people—I played with senior players, older than me, and they were sometimes drinking and what. But I never drank beer myself. I was just enjoying sweet beer, that which they made, until I got married. I was very much devoted to, married to, music. Yes.

MC: Can you think of what was the most important, the most special, the best moment you can think of as far as your music? What was the best performance you ever had? The most exciting experience? Can you think of one of those?

CM: Since I've gone through a lot of performances in different places, I don't forget when we performed at Africa Center in London. We really played very, very well, and that was our first appearance—Mhuri Yekwa Rwizi. The first mbira ensemble to get there, so I was very much touched by how everybody in our group ended our performance—with the new audience who did not know much about that kind of music. It was difficult to really know what people were thinking about our music—their responses—so it was very challenging. It was very successful because that was when we started getting some more invitations.

MC: Very good! That sounds like a real highlight. I was thinking, since I'm interviewing you here in California, and all of the others that I've interviewed were in Zimbabwe; I was either in their home or at the College of Music. Mostly in their homes, so it felt really comfortable for them to be in their own space, their own country—what they're familiar with. Whereas here, you're in a strange place, you know? Do you feel comfortable in California? Would it be a lot better if I was interviewing you in your home? Would it feel quite different?

CM: That's a very good question. It is indeed a very challenging thing, but as far as I'm concerned, I even feel at home here, because of the hospitality given to me by people and I regard that as the beginning of constructing a musical bridge and cultural bridge as well, so this is why I strongly feel being at home here.

MC: You know, we talk so much in America, about cross-cultural links, and multicultural—the special thing is, here we are experiencing that—we're doing it! Do you practice your instrument now? Like, you're getting ready to perform here. Will you be practicing what you're going to be performing? Is practice a part of what you do?

CM: Yes, when I'm going to perform I really have to know what songs I'm going to play, what type of performance is it, because certain things are situational. First I have to know what I'm going to do. Am I going for a workshop? Am I going for a bira, a traditional ceremony? So then I have to be geared up accordingly. I need some time to go through what I'm going to play, so that I have a sense of it before I'm in front of the crowd.

MC: Yea. I want to choose my question carefully. I'm really interested in improvisation. When you do your performance, do you improvise, and if so how do you think about that? What is improvisation to you?

CM: As far as I'm concerned, because the songs which we play are traditional, they are songs which I cannot claim to have the right of composition, or having composed them, because they are inherited. As far as improvisations are concerned, sometimes you come up with, as you play, as an experienced player, there are certain things that happen during the process of playing. Some things may be good, some may not be good. Or I might—my finger, or my thumb might touch on a certain key, or what have you, and then I happen to like that key, so then I add that to my repertoire. But there might be also something which may not be good. Then I have to throw away what is not good and bring in what is good. When I'm teaching I have to tell my students, this is how I learned it first, but this is what I also improvised. Because you gain experience, and when gaining experience, you also expand yourself. So that is the way I do some improvisations.

MC: Right. Do you suppose that when you're playing tomorrow night that something might happen that you've never done before? You might like it, and might keep that idea? It could happen?

CM: It could happen. This is a traditional instrument and certain things may come to you at a certain time when you don't expect it to happen, and then they start happening and you have to accommodate that.

MC: I think that's what lends that special character to improvisation. You never know exactly what might happen. Whereas for classical pianists, we pretty much know how Bach wanted it, or how Beethoven wants it, and sure, we can make it more interesting with our dynamics and that sort of thing, but we can't change the notes; you can change the notes, and I can, when we improvise. I hope I'm understanding you right. Is it partly that when you're teaching a song to your student or to a class, you want them to learn it as it was created, as it was composed. You want them to learn it that way first and then they can maybe start changing something a little bit. Maybe they could improvise and do their own little change, but they should learn it as it is? Is that what you're saying?

CM: Yes, that's what I'm saying. When I teach I would really like people to play exactly what I've taught them, then they can also impart that the same way I did. I'm trying to preserve the really original way—how it was. So if somebody teaches something you have to honor it. This is what I did, because I'm a strong believer in wanting to preserve the music as well as the culture.

MC: That's very helpful, what you just said, because that makes me aware of how careful a person like me, who doesn't really know these songs well, how careful I need to be if I want to change some things. I better know that song well first, before I start playing around with it.

CM: And also, another tip I can give is that it's important also for musicians to discuss opinions, to come together. If you have composed something, play before a seasoned player and say, "What do you think about this? Comments really help. That's what I do if I have someone who is coming to me, and has started doing it. I also involve some seasoned players and start playing it. Sometimes I don't tell them anything, I just play it. I'm wanting their comments and then they will comment, "Ah, I like that," or, "Ah, that doesn't sound good."

MC: We do that with classical music too. When I'm teaching my students, then they have to play it for some other piano faculty, and they say, "No, don't do it that way, do it this way." They have some other opinions about how that piece should be played, so there's a similar thing going on in classical music, which I think is kind of interesting. I have a question for you about tuning. At first when Ephat and I were playing together, and I was playing on the piano at the College of Music, he would bring in various mbiras. He would bring in his dza vadzimu and some others—nyunga nyunga, and some others. And sometimes I would think, it sounds alright with piano. Other times I would think, "Oh, it's not in tune, and it's bothering my ear," and I was worrying about that. When I was listening to these recordings of our improvisations and thinking about making a CD, I was thinking, "Is this going to be right, that these tunings sound to my ear, kind of off?" Do you know the name Bruno Nettl? Do you know that name?

CM: No.

MC: He's considered to be a world famous ethnomusicologist, and he was teaching this class at the University of Washington on improvisation. So I brought a tape of Ephat and myself playing and I played it for him, and I said, "What do you think about this tuning problem?" And he said, "Don't worry about it. This is an interesting thing you're doing putting this western instrument together with this African instrument—it's an interesting sound."

CM: Right. My comment to that would be when we were playing in Mhuri Yekwa Rwizi we used to have four different tunings—four different mbiras. We used to have a "gandanga", that's the name we call it ourselves, because it's a discordant kind of thing, you're talking about. That mbira tuning is good on certain songs, and on certain songs it's not good. Or when you want to use it, you really need to choose the song which goes with the instrument. We had the dza vadzimu tuning, and there were two kinds of low, very low tunings, which we consider as the same as Nyamaropa tuning, although it is not all that low. The only difference is a gandanga, which is discordant, so those songs used to have different tunings. Each time Mr. Mudi, our leader, used to say, "Today, guys, can we play on such a tuning?" Then we start playing, and it can change in the evening during a ceremony. He would say, "Can you get the standard tuning or whatever," and then we get the other tuning and start playing, and that helps also. Musicians have to be conversant with any tuning.

MC: It makes sense what you're saying, even though I didn't know very much about it. Some pianos I would be playing on, or with certain mbiras, would sound really nice with certain songs, so what you're saying makes a lot of sense.

CM: Thank you.

MC: But, I'm sensing that I need to study, I need to know more about tunings. I think Paul Berliner's book, "Soul of Mbira," would be a good place for me to do some more reading to understand, because tunings is a complex, complicated thing to know about, isn't it?

CM: Yes, it is. Also it's important on the part of a musician to know the tuning, when the key's out of tune. It's really important.

MC: I'm starting to know that on my instrument, dza vadzimu, and on my nyunga nyunga mbira from Eastern Zimbabwe. I studied the latter mbira with Dumi Maraire in Seattle and, that one, I can tell clearly if it's out of tune, or not. Do you know Steve Golovnin?

CM: Yes, I know him.

MC: He tuned this one for me (dza vadzimu). (I showed my instrument to Cosmas). This was made by Fradreck and Sam Mujuru.

CM: (He plays). Yea, it's one of the low tunings, but there are others which is lower than this which is played by the Mujuru's. They do have another one which is lower than this. The other piece of advice I want to give you is getting to know the beat of the song. It's important for the person who is playing the mbira to know where the beat is. It's important for the mbira player to know how to play hosho.

MC: How do you teach them to feel that beat? Where do you start?

CM: I start when I give them lessons on the beat e.g. "Can you clap?" I demonstrate to them and they get to know. They should have a feel of what they are doing first. That helps them, you know? Whatever they'll be learning.

(We talked about the Tonga, music of the Binga area, and Cosmos liked very much the idea of preserving that music—as Bryan Paul suggested in his interview).

MC: Also, at the College of Music now, they're offering quite a lot of jazz classes and they're offering some Latino, I think it is—dance. In other words, they're opening up to, and encouraging the students there, especially the black students, to be open to other music from other cultures.

CM: Which is very good. I like that.

MC: Yea, but first of all, I think their high priority is that their students would understand and be able to teach their own music—mbira, the drumming of course, the hoshos. So Zimbabwean music is first, and then being open to musics from other cultures. What I noticed in several interviews, Stella Chiweshe said it, and Bryan Paul, maybe some others, they wished so much they had had a chance to do some piano—training in piano. Do you feel that way?

CM: Yes. You know we just did not have all those facilities, all those things, but they are really good. That's why my kids are very much into music. They are interested in western type of instruments, although, of course, they have been learning what I do. Coming back to this Binga thing, I strongly feel very much touched, and I wish people can afford to get to write about that music because it might easily get into extinction when old players are dying these days, and a lot of things happening. So that really needs to be captured and noted down. Because, from my experiences, I worked in that area. I was based in Wankie as a manager for Dairy Marketing Board. I was in that area for about seven years, so I've known the people who live in that area, how they live. So I strongly feel it is important to do that. Now I'm interested in this kind of connection between culture and music. I'm very much interested in that and that is why again I think it is important for me to let you know that's why I left the Dairy Marketing Board after twenty years.

MC: Do you think of yourself first as a performer? You also sound like you're a music educator.

CM: Well, you are the one who can tell, you are trained. I enjoy working with ethnomusicologists. I believe we should work hand in glove—musicians and ethnomusicologists.

MC: Yes. So you really have at least three hats—a performer, a music educator, an ethnomusicologist (C laughs heartily). Of course you're a father and a husband and so on.

CM: Thank you.

MC: Do you have some dream for the future that you hope to accomplish or are you quite happy with how things are moving for you and you just hope for the same?

CM: Well, my wish would be that we could have more. If I could have a chance to go to more universities, colleges where I can be showing people—having workshops—really help out and use my talent, share with some willing students, that is really my wish. It's very expensive. I can't afford to—like paying for myself an air ticket like this time. If we could get some sponsorship to be able to go to places where I can have a chance of teaching.

Also, my wish is to work with more of the people I am dealing with from the States—it's a multicultural thing. I want to see them coming back and perform before Zimbabweans, and Zimbabweans coming to perform in America and get to see what has been happening in America where I've been visiting, teaching mbira. This is why, in the Nhimbe Project (Nhimbe for Progress, working to improve sub-standard living conditions and provide educational opportunities), which I'm doing with Jaiaen Beck, we're wanting to introduce musicians, people like you coming to Zimbabwe, and going to schools. I want you to say something to school children, show them mbira and marimbas, because a lot of our children are now being driven by seeing westerners playing mbiras, and now they are coming back to their roots, emulating. So that's why I wish you could come back and do that, and see more Zimbabweans doing what they are supposed to do culturally.

BEAULER DYOKO

Interviewing Beauler Dyoko was a challenge, but a most interesting experience for me. I had observed her play mbira at the Zimbabwe College of Music in 1994 when I was teaching at the College, and found her to be intense, colorful and fun to watch. I knew that she was a very good mbira player, but communicating with her was intimidating to me because her English was so limited, so I did not even try. She seemed to come from a different world than I knew, but this intrigued me.

For the interview in 2001 in Seaside, California, I was afraid that her English would be very difficult to understand. And I was fairly certain that hers would be an unusual story. As it turned out, I enjoyed visiting with Beauler and, since the interview was on tape, I knew that I could get help in transcribing it if needed. She clearly is an individualist, and was driven to be an mbira player in spite of serious obstacles—family and tradition.

She has a very attractive face, a good sense of humor and a great smile! She seemed to me to have one foot in traditional music and one foot in the twenty-first century. There is a savvy, clever side to Beauler in certain things. But she is seriously limited by her lack of English, when performing and teaching in the States. Fortunately Cosmas Magaya is very willing to help her.

Beauler is a caring person as evidenced by her assuming the care of ten children in her family, whose parents have died of AIDS. She is wisely working with a network of women in the U.S. who are helping her with money and clothes for her children. Beauler is working to improve the status of Zimbabwean women, a noble and much-needed cause in Zimbabwe now.

Myrna Capp: We could start with where you're from originally.

Beauler Dyoko: I was born in Harare, Zimbabwe. My father is from Portugal. Mother, she's from Mozambique. Now I was born in 1945, 23 November. My father passed away in 1951. I went to school in St. Peters in Harare, St. Peters school. I didn't go for further education. I go for Standard Five. My mother, she had no money to pay for me. Then I just left in 1959—I had my husband. We had two children, and from that two children we did get married in a Catholic church, but we didn't stay married long. I caught him red-handed with another girl. I left him and I went back to my mother and stayed with my mother with the children. But he came back to my mother to come

and collect the children. They took the children. My brother says, "Don't worry, you're still young, you can make more children."

But you must know that children don't forget their mother. They will come back to you. In the 1960's I start getting sick. I was dreaming of mbira. I told my mother, "Mommie, I'm dreaming of playing mbira." She said, "Yea, we can play mbira, but not a woman. A woman doesn't play mbira." I said "I'm dreaming about it." She said, "Our church, they're Catholic, they don't like mbira." Well I stayed getting sick, I was very sick, I was so thin. I went to the hospital with Mommie. The Dr. says that he can't see any sickness in my body. "She's ok. Maybe she's only thinking too much, but she's ok—can't see anything." We went back, but my body was very sore. I was real ill. I kept on telling Mommie that I want some mbira. Mommie refused. Then I disappeared for ten months. I went to the rural area called Chipureru. Now called Guruwe. I was there for ten months. They gave me treatment from a vadzimu herbalist. In the eleventh month, my mother, she was looking for me. I mean, from the time I disappeared, my mother, she was looking for me. She went to the hospitals, police, mortuaries, she didn't find me. She thought maybe I'm dead. She wore a black cloak and dress.

Well, the eleventh month I went back home. Twas in the morning— 7:00 a.m. the buses which we took were area buses. I seen my mother, she was basking in the sun. She was looking where the buses come from and she seen me coming with a basket full of herbs, a walking stick, "possessing." I was "possessing." My father, he was the one coming to me, he was the one who was playing mbira. Now when she was seeing me coming, first thing, she was scared. She thought I'm a spook, I'm a ghost. I went straight to her, and looked at her. At first I see that she's scared, but I sat near her; she wanted to run away. I said, "No Mommie, it's me." Then she said, where you coming from?" I said, the bush. She says, "In the bush? I says, "Yea." She said, "Are you ok?" I said, "No. I brought things here in the basket finally." She opened the basket—she finds these herbs there and a walking stick. And she was surprised and I said, "What's wrong?" Her mother thought: "But if I say you're not allowed to do it...maybe she'll disappear, she'll disappear for good, or she'll throw herself out in the water in the river."

Now I told her I'm still dreaming about mbira and I told her also that I went to Guruwe and they fixed me—the spirit what was worrying me. I'm no more sick, but I still want to play on the mbira. She says, "Ok, which spirit is that?" I say, "I don't know, I must ask him." I didn't want to tell her. Then she said, "How can we call that spirit? I said, "We can pour water, and put it upside down. The light in one must go up, the smoking one must go down. And she did it. Then the spirit came—they ask each other. The spirit says, "I came to my daughter. I'm her last born. I can't go to the person who is not strong. They can't keep me. They won't keep my rules. That's why I chose the young girl." *(Her mother wanted to prove that her daughter, Beauler, was for sure getting possessed by her late husband, by summoning the spirit to possess Beauler, so that she could directly discuss with it how they courted and so on. So they brewed traditional beer and held that ceremony;* explained by Cosmas Magaya).

Then Mommie says, "No, I want to know that it's you"; and then the spirits and her mother were telling each other that you know where I married, I did like that and that and that, and Mommie says it's true, it's my husband. She agreed now. Then the spirit said that I want some (some what?) We must brew some beer. Then I called some friends of mine, and said you must meet them. And Mommie says, "Ok, we'll do it."

The spirits went away and I told my mother, "I want you to buy me an mbira. Yea, I want to buy mbira but I've got no money." Her mother said, "The person that's possessing you, it's your father." I said, "Oh," but Beauler's mother didn't say no. She just said, "I've got no money to buy mbira." Now the spirit was a man. He was going far away, but he was selling mbira for money. Now something made the spirit pull to my mother—he was selling this mbira. He said, "I don't want money. I want some salt for trading. Then my mother says, "How much salt do you want?" He says, well, a cup—a teacup—that one. She took the salt, and put it in the cup and gave him and he gave me the mbira. *(After the spirit had dispossessed Beauler, she insisted on her mother buying her an mbira. At this point her mother had been convinced that Beauler was being possessed by her husband and agreed to buy her an mbira by barter deal with a man who was selling salt. The man agreed to exchange a full tea cup of salt for an mbira. Beauler thinks the spirit played a role in the coming of this salt man; Cosmas Magaya.)*

BD: So I put that mbira away—like a pillow. I started dreaming playing "Nhemamusasa", "Bande Tirera", and "Bugatiende". And I played in the morning—I got up, I went and sit on the shed, on peachie tree shed. And Mommie, she came there, and found I'm playing mbira, and says, "Sure that your father is real on you, your father was playing mbira, now you're playing mbira." She said, "Maybe that's it; oh well, I can't even say no. Anything you want from me I will do for you." And then I said Mommie, I want to go and record." "She say, oh, you aren't going to record. Only a few weeks you started playing mbira." "I say, yea, I want to go and record." She said, "You'll disgrace us. You go that side, you won't play nicely." I said, "I'll try." Another man who plays mbira, a man who makes the bricks, he's a brick maker, I called him. He didn't say no. We went to the broadcasting place. Just recorded two songs. Then they gave us L40 (British pounds) and I went back home. I showed Mommie the money, she says, "Ha, such a lot of money. How many songs did you play?" I said, "I just played two songs." She said, "You can keep on playing." "This thing's got money. You must keep on playing it." I said, "Yea, I can play."

From that time it was 1962-63, I started recording good songs. In '63, '64 I was playing mbira in the bira ceremony. In '65 I did record the other record, a single, that, I played. Now, l967, twas hot, the war it was started now. Fighting—Ian Smith. They seemed to say, "We don't want you people—you people who play mbira." They refused to allow that recording to be played. They said, "You're giving power to those people fighting in the bush. We don't want you again to play mbira." We stopped until 1980's. And in '80 the war was finished. I went again to record and I got some albums and then the other album, the last one, I recorded in 1992. It's called "Babamyaradzi." The flip side it's "Mongovira." And from then they were saying, she's mad, she's playing mbira. She won't cook good food. But I'm cooking better food than those that don't play mbira. Here in America, I've got friends, made friends, while those people that were saying that mbira's not good for the women, they asking me to play with them. I say, "No, no, no. This is not for the men, it's for the women."

MC: So you were one of the first women to really get that going, that women can play; it's alright for women to play?

BD: Yes. 1962.

MC: Stella Chiweshe came later then?

BD: Stella came...something like... '65 or '70.

MC: And now Chiwoniso Maraire is promoting that women can play, right, and do all kinds of things?

BD: Yes.

MC: Do you know Chi?

BD: Chiwoniso...yes. Dumisani Maraire's daughter.

MC: And I'm reading that she's doing some mbira, jazz kinds of things; have you heard her do that at all?

BD: In Zimbabwe there's no mbira jazz. For the spirit, for the people asking for rain to come, traditional Zimbabwean mbira only! Not for the jazz; maybe it's western mbira, that. Not Zimbabwe mbira.

MC: Well, she lived in Seattle and so she became westernized. It sounds like there was no other music in your family, like your mother, obviously was not a musician...but your father was a mbira player, and you have children.

BD: Yea, I've got four children.

MC: Are they doing mbira?

BD: Two girls they don't play mbira, those are someone's property because they're married. Two boys, that's the boys who go away. They both play mbira. The young one he plays drums and mbira. I've got my own instrument. I bought it in 1999. Now I've got a group...fourteen people. Three guitars, organ, trumpet, saxophone, four mbira players, hosho and drum. Three girls dancing.

MC: So would you say your home base is Harare?

BD: Yes, it's reaching to Chitungwiza,

MC: So your group plays just around Harare mostly? Or do you travel some?

(Yes, the group plays in Harare and in other parts of the country; Cosmas Magaya.)

BD: The first group, my first group—we were only four; four of us—two women, two guys; my son and another boy; one woman and another guy, they passed away with Aids. Then I took this new group. The first group, I did a tour with them. First tour in Finland, from there went to Malaysia, then from there went to South Africa. From South Africa, came back here in Zimbabwe and we start getting sick. All of them, two of them passed away. And I took this new group in '94. Well, I still got them. We performed in Parliament in Harare, opening of Parliament, other shows. These are shows we did or are still doing. I even composed a song called, "Nosofa, Munosofa." It was about you'll die with Aids.

My niece passed away with Aids. She left ten children. I'm keeping them. There's nobody at her home where she was married. Her husband passed away before her, then my niece left ten children. She died in my house. She was in the hospital. They say we can't keep her in the hospital, she's got that kind of sickness, Aids. Otherwise she will die before time. "Can you keep your niece at home? You can do home care." And I did keep her, and she died in my house. She left those children with me.

MC: It must have felt overwhelming.

BD: It's even choking me. Now they're in school. They were very sick. They had belharzia. And they had worms in the stomach. Some of the worms they were coming out the nose. Then I went to the doctor with them. The doctor gave me some medicine. I gave them and those worms came out, all of them. And then the belharzia, it's ok now. Then I went and I put them in school. I need someone to help me. I need someone to help me.

MC: I think so. Do you have some help?

BD: Yea, some people from here, women from here did help me. Some of them, they giving me clothes for those children.

MC: Wow, that's an overwhelming story. And I understand that that's going on a lot.

BD: In Zimbabwe they're dying like chickens. Ah, this Aids business. Maybe God is punishing people. They're doing...ten women, ten men...

MC: Do you teach some?

BD: Yea, I do teach mbira.

MC: Is your favorite to teach individual lessons, or do you like to teach small classes?

BD: I do teach any. I think it's in my blood now.

MC: Do you teach the songs just as you learned them? Do you want your students to learn them just as they are or do you like them to make some changes and do improvisation, or how do you do it?

BD: No, because these songs...no one taught me. No. I can't make them. They must change. (Beauler likes people to learn her songs. She likes her students to make some changes and do improvisations *to her songs and she says she teaches orally—teacher and student side by side; Cosmas).* They must learn my song. I don't teach a song with notes (notation). I teach song playing there and showing the student how to strike the keys by rote.

MC: And when I was in your class last year in Eugene at the Zimbabwe Music Festival, I noticed repeating—repetition—is the way you teach a lot, isn't it?

BD: Yea. Even singing, I teach singing. Clapping.

MC: Is it important? How do you teach them to feel the beat? Is that important to you?

BD: Yea, you must feel the beat and then you know how to play the song, to sing the song.

MC: So do you get them to clap, or how to you get them to feel the beat?

BD: Yea, to clap. I play mbira for them. I play mbira and then I give them the beat with my leg.

MC: Right, when you're actually performing yourself. Well, first I want to start with practice—do you practice? Will you be practicing today or tomorrow for some performances here at the Festival?

BD: Yea, tonight we'll practice a few songs. Some of them—because we always play the songs—can't play a new song. We'll play other songs which is good for the audience.

MC: And would you play songs here that you would play in Zimbabwe? Or are you trying to do certain songs here so that people here can learn them very well, they need to hear them more?

BD: They must learn. If you want to play mbira, you must learn Zimbabwe mbira, you can't learn States mbira. (B laughs heartily) I don't know how they play it here. You play the African mbira in Zimbabwe, Zimbabwe mbira ...you don't change it.

MC: And would you and Cosmas play the Zimbabwean songs—would you play them the same as he would?

BD: Yea.

MC: And then would you maybe—after you get going and into it, and you might find a new note or something you like and you might change it a little bit?

BD: Yea; it goes with what you're playing. It's good.

MC: So there's some spontaneity there; something new could happen, because in the performance that happens, doesn't it? Something different might happen. It's ok.

BD: Yea, you know, I compose my songs like we're conversing, good stories, and then I go somewhere. I see other people fighting or what, and then I will put it together. I play the song about that which is happening in an area.

MC: That's makes sense. You have to know your audience. You have to know what's going on around the area. So I'm sitting here in California interviewing you, whereas for the other nine, I was interviewing them in their homes in Harare, or, like Oliver, outside of Harare, near Norton. And it feels different to be here, doesn't it? It's not the same at all.

BD: No it's not.

MC: How do you feel about that? It's ok?

BD: Oh, it's ok, but I'm learning more—I'm learning more. These other things which I didn't know before, now I can ...I know how to do it. About we women—we play mbira; other women they're so fast they can catch onto mbira so fast. In Zimbabwe, you don't see people wanting to play mbira. You can say now, this is for the spirit, you can play mbira for the spirit, you see? But they want guitars in Zimbabwe...they used to play mbira. They like the new instrument. Guitars. Now here in the States they want a new instrument, that's mbira.

MC: Sounds familiar. Could you tell me the most difficult, the biggest problem you've had in performance, or a funny story—anything to do with a difficult thing you were in, or one of your good, happy, one of your best experiences?

BD: Yea, it's true. That's a good question, that. Like the time I was playing mbira. I was playing mbira, all mbira acoustic. I wanted to put mbira and guitars together because our children they don't want mbira, they want guitars. Now I wanted to tell them that they must know mbira, it's good. But they don't ask for mbira, they ask for guitars. Now I was asking the guys whose instrument was guitars, "Please can you play together with mbira." They didn't want me to play with them, no. They make us disgraced for the dza vadzimu— people drinking beer to become "possessed." I say no they don't "possess." Don't think that vadzimu come for nothing. If you ask them to come they can come, but if you just play for an audience they don't come. We want our culture to come back. We musn't lose our culture. Those people with guitars, they didn't want to preserve our culture.

Then there's another band with Jona Story, they were called "African Help." We were doing combined shows. People were coming in to that show. Now I thought, if you can put an amplifier on your mbira—it will be like a guitar. I did put a speaker on mbira. Now I didn't know where to get the amplifiers. I was using the alum watch, the engine of it. It's like a plate, a round one. I told my son, take off this, buy some string, cords, tie there by that. There's two things—just weld them nicely and you stick it on the mbira, and then you put it on the amplifier. Then it started, it was like the guitar! Now people, they want it. I said "No, this speaker is not from me, I didn't buy it here. Go look at the speakers there in the music shop." Then they go there—find the speakers, it's $1,500. They can't afford to buy it, and I used the watch for $9!

From there people say, "We want mbira, we want mbira," because I put that electric to the mbira. Now children, young guys, new generation, they wanted now to come and play mbira. From there I had a real good mbira; I had a show here, they called me here. First show with Mhuri Yedwa Rwizi and Cosmas, together. We did play here, then I went back and went and buy my own instrument. Now those people, that are saying, they didn't want me to play with them, now they say, "Please can we hire you?" I say no, this is mbira instrument, you can't hire (rent) my mbira instrument 'cause this is others you possessed." They say, we want some guitars. I say no, this guitar is for mbira. You can't take this guitar because there's possessing. I'm not hiring this mbira! You don't hire my instrument because you people, you didn't want me to combine with you. Now you want...I don't want!" That's the thing what was worrying me in my lifetime. Now I'm ok.

MC: Do you have a bad experience to tell me about? Or a funny story? Something that was really difficult for you in a performance, or just anything? Your hardest times?

BD: The hardest time is like this, I've got that instrument and no car. Maybe it's raining— some people called me, and I'm all over to look for the car to rent. Sometimes they say we want $2,500. I give them, they say, "Oh you came late, I lose my job."

MC: So you really need a car.

BD: Now I need a car.

MC: The most difficult thing.

BD: I've got a *big* house. I bought now, I bought the house. I had no good house. My mother's house it was so crowded. I was...together... those ten children. God helped me and vadzimu helped me, the women of America they did—donated some few money. They gave me and then I go buy the house for $350,000. I'm not yet there. I'm still maintaining, but...

MC: But you'll be coming there; you're looking forward to it, I think.

BD: Yes.

MC: What is your dream for the next five years, or just for the next part of your life? What is your dream, what do you most hope for, what do you want to have happen for you? Are you happy with how things are going now? Or do you have a dream?

BD: The thing what I want—I don't dream for anything; if I say I dream something, it comes through the spirit. Now these days, I just ask— please God and my spirit—can you help me? These children to grow up nicely. Maybe if I'm old they will keep me.

MC: It's something we all have to consider. You seem to me, that your religion is very important in everything you're doing. Do you mean the ancestral spirit, as you say—God? How do you speak of religion for you? I can tell it's important to you.

BD: Ah...I speak like how that herbalist made me to ...keep me...to cure my sickness through this spirit. I can take some water, kneel down and talk to my father and in my father, my grandpa, my mother's grandpa, my mother's father, and mother, all those, I tell them that—can you help me with such a thing? You know where to go—ask—eating hot things, talking rough to people, you are dead. Can you put these words what I'm telling you to our forefather, our God? But if you talk like that, they'll put it to them, put it to his father, his grandpa—go straight to God. That's what our children are asking for, because you can't talk to God without his ministers. God is ministers, it's your ancestors. And it's true, you can't go to George Bush straight away without seeing his ministers. You'll get shot!

MC: It's true. I noticed you weren't mentioning the Roman Catholics in all of this.

GC: Was the Catholic church important in your life?

BD: Yea, because I was brought up in the Catholic church. The Catholic church, they don't say that you musn't cure people. I'm a herbalist. I throw bones as a fortune teller, I cure people, I play mbira. If I want to come here, first, to see a priest and say, "Please can you bless my mbira?" then he will bless it. In the Catholic church they say, if you want to ask, maybe someone died there. Your great grandpa—there's a child coming there. Then the grandpa knows where to go and put the body? If she was nice, or maybe he was not nice—he'll know where he can put them.

MC: Do you have anything else you want to add that I didn't think to ask you about?

BD: Yea, I want more women to play mbira. I want more women to play mbira, children—they must play mbira. We musn't lose our culture. Like this now, I'm old. If I die without teaching others with my talent. If I teach my friends, or my children—young children, those mbira will still go ahead. If I do a bad heart, no, I musn't teach people, because it's my composition—that's a bad heart. If you die, you've got no history to talk to, to talk about you. I rather do that, because these things—it's not my own—it's for everybody. We must teach each other. Sometimes, I'll say to someone, can you teach me organ? Or piano? It's that way...you can teach me.

Because God says that me, I am teaching in the States, and people say, why are we playing mbira, mbira is not from our culture? God created two people on earth, a man and a woman. From there he didn't create color, he just made two people. There's no black, there's no white, no green, there's no yellow. One person, two people only. Now the mbira music is for everybody—not for one person. God made trees like that tree, that is one there, got one trunk and so many branches. The bush got so many flowers, that's how God made us here. He made us in colors, that this world must be pretty, but we are one person. We can cut our blood here. I cut your blood—it is the same...there's no green blood, there's no white blood.... It's all same! We are all one. That's why mbira it's all over. I went to China—they liked mbira. Yea, I went to Malaysia, they liked mbira. I teach the Malasia mbira. I went to Portugal, I teach mbira. There in Holland I teach the mbira. Mbira is for everybody. It was a small instrument. Maybe they thought that they didn't want—there's no good voice there. Now you put that electric...you can hear it 3 kilometers.

MC: Opened up a whole new world!

FARAI GEZI

Farai Gezi's love of music has its roots in his family lineage, especially his parents. At one time his father taught at a reformatory and befriended the reformatory students, who were from all over Zimbabwe. The students would come to the Gezi's home to do music and Farai was deeply influenced by them. Also, his mother was from the Makeba family, known for the renowned South African musician, Miriam Makeba.

Farai was fortunate to receive a solid music education at Kwanangoma School in Bulawayo, where he studied African music, as well as Western music, particularly piano and flute. Although Farai's parents were against his having a career in music, he, through an interesting turn of events, joined the military band, introducing marimba and mbira, Western music theory, and use of African songs in the band repertoire. In his own way, he was an ethnomusicologist, doing cultural preservation!

Training Zimbabwean cultural officers in music, art, painting, and so on, was one of his contributions at one point in his career. He had a passion for educating rural Zimbabwean children, since he believed that rural kids did not have the same opportunities, especially in the arts, as urban kids. As a result, Farai started Chipawo (Children's Performing Arts Workshop), which has grown considerably.

I wish I might have visited Farai's backyard marimba workshop, where people came from Japan, the U.S., and elsewhere to learn to build marimbas. His description of it made it sound like a stimulating place to learn and work with a variety of people, in spite of using primitive, very basic tools. His diverse career includes doing workshops, performing, teaching and consulting in music. Farai's vision of an integrated arts school in Harare, including music, art, dance, theatre, music therapy, teacher education, science, and so on, was inspiring. Farai is an example of a Zimbabwean musician thinking "outside of the box." I hope his vision will come to fruition.

Through my participation in Zimfest, the Zimbabwe Music Festival that occurs in the Western U.S. every summer, I learned of Farai's involvement in mediating cultural politics. He felt strongly that festivals celebrating Zimbabwean music should remain as true as possible to what Zimbabwean music was in the past (traditional), but more importantly to him, what Zimbabwean music is now. He believed that the music should not be sentimentalized, spiritualized, and emotionally charged, without full understanding of it. Going back to the musical roots in Zimbabwe was what Farai advocated, if economically feasible (e.g., having the Festival in Harare). Because of the current economic and political climate in Zimbabwe, that may not happen any time in the near future. Perhaps there are other ways of addressing these issues so important to Farai.

Myrna Capp: Let's start out with where you're from originally.

Farai Gezi: I was born in Motoko, the northeastern direction of Zimbabwe. My mother is a South African, from the Makeba family. The Xhosa people. My mother is from the Makeba family. That is the Xhosa, Miriam Makeba, well-known South African musician. My father is a Zulu, and Zimbabwean. I was born in the northeastern part of the country, in a place called Motoko, 23 January, 1949, that's when I was born. My mother then was nursing; was at the hospital as a nurse, and my father was a teacher in some of the Methodist missionary schools. So we moved from there to many other places. But the most important place that really sort of triggered off my interest in music was when we were in Kadoma. It's just before Gweru. My father was teaching at what we call a reformatory, what is now called correctional centers for problem kids. He was very friendly to those kids and they used to come to our house. Somehow I learned quite a lot of music from these kids. They came from many different parts of the country.

So we saw some concerts, kids concerts, and I learned many musical things from them. Also my father had his own quartet that he used to sing with. We were treated as sort of the junior, incoming quartet, and so we learned a lot of songs from him and also learned about singing. The church also contributed toward my music development. I loved to be in choir. The first days, I didn't like to be in the choir, but my mother somehow pushed me into the choir, and she used to always check with the choir teacher, to make sure I was attending the choir. So then I started just to like it. Also, I think the encouragement of my father and the encouragement of my mother, it really contributed towards more of my appreciating it. I wasn't sure though, of becoming a music practitioner as such. I wasn't sure at that stage, because we talked, my family, at one point. I wanted to be a train driver. That's the thing I really loved to do. Even up to today. Sometimes I say to myself, "Why didn't I become a train driver?"

After that I went to high school. At high school we had our own band, a pop band. Of course in the end there were some problems. We nearly chugged away (dropped out) from high school. But some people intervened and somehow we were saved. But the principal of the school said, "No more." The group are disbanded. So we said we'd disband, but on holidays we could meet. When I finished high school, my younger brother somehow was ahead of me in school. Because I had some problems when I was, I think, in Standard 3. I didn't do well. My brother caught up with me. You know you spend a lot of time in music so things added up with him being a little bit ahead of me. After high school he was ahead of me, and when he finished, he then went to the College of Education in Bulawayo, where there is this Kwonangoma College.

Then he thought of me and said, "I think, since he's so deep into music, I think he better get some formal training so that he can work in schools and maybe be of help." So he wrote me and I took this letter to my parents and they agreed. I went into this College in 1973. Then I met the late Mr. Olaf Axelson. He was a Swedish missionary, of the Lutheran church. Also another person who really played a VERY important part in my life was Alport Mhla/Mushlang. So these two they were important mentors to me. Olaf Axelson was the head for Kwanongoma, and Alport M was his deputy. I think most of the really deep, the heart of my development was because of these two people, and I, even up to today, I look upon them with all the respect that I can in my life. They really changed me completely, a turn around of my life. I was at Kwanongoma where we were doing both African and European music. I studied at Kwanangoma, I studied mbira, both the nyunga nyunga and dza vadzimu, and also the African drums and also folk music, African music. Also we did marimba and we had to do composition and creative playing, improvisation.

All THAT we did. Then on the European instruments I did my piano up to about grade 8 level, then my flute was also up to grade 8 level. I learned to play the flute initially and then learned the saxophone; the fingering is more or less the same. From there, after I had graduated, where to go was now a bit of a problem. The government stopped employing music teachers into the local system. That was '75, '76. Yea, they stopped doing that because they thought it was all about politics. The white government was sort of scared. They didn't want the idea of culturalization of the people, maintaining the traditional culture.

They had to cut us off. Then I said, "Oh, now I think I'm stuck. So now what are my parents going to say?" because they had warned me many, many years ago that this sort of thing could happen. They said, "You'll never get very far," and when I got there I said, "Oh, there it is again, that thing has caught up with me." So there was a vacancy in the military band, the army, and I think I was the most highly qualified person who applied. When my application got to the army band there was a gentleman who also did a lot in my music area. He was called Major McDonald and was of Scottish origin. He was in the Rhodesian army at that time, and the army was shunned by all blacks, and especially people my age. Now I had to go through this hard thing. I thought, "Look, I have to get employment." My parents told me that this thing will not take you very far, at the same time there is this political pressure on me. What then do I do?

So I quietly applied for this job without telling anyone, and I got this job. Major McDonald drove the army land rover, straight to Kwanangoma College of music, in front of all these kids, and he went to Mr. Axelson and said, "I'd like to talk to Farai." I said, "Oh, what'll I do." I couldn't say, Why did you come in an army land rover?" I couldn't say that there. He talked to me in a private room, and he said clearly he was aware of the political pressure, and the political problems. But he said to me, just know that in five years time this country will be ok and you will still be needed. Yea, you will still be needed. So just when he said that, that is why I made up my mind. He said, as soon as you finish school, you are graduating this year, as soon as you finish, come straight away. So I had to go after graduation. Then I said no, I need about two months to go back home, sort out my things, then say goodbye to my family. So I did that, and he said, no problem, you can come in after the new year, the second or first week in January. I said fine, so I went in after the new year, second/first week in January.

When I got there they also called me for another interview. Regulations are that before you start teaching here you have to be trained. I said, now where are we going. He said, "No, no, no, don't worry, people with special skills—you just go in for six weeks. It's part of the regulation. So I had to go in for six weeks, but I sort of enjoyed the company. I also met other people from other colleges that were teachers and so it made me a little bit settled down. After the six weeks then I started working with the army band, and at that point I also introduced marimba into their system, and I also introduced mbira. Major McDonald really approved of that. So even up to now—I left many years ago—now in that context, military band, I want to teach them theory from about grade one to about at least grade three, grade four, those who wanted to write examinations. They did examinations in grade five and some at grade eight. I was working also with arrangements of songs, taking African songs, writing them for the military band and I also was a member of the dance band. I was with that for about eight years and into Independence. I then decided to go into civilian life. We are doing music now, in the ministry of sport and culture, where I established a music training program for cultural officers. We were having this, at what used to be called Mount Hampden Art Training Center, where we specialized in music and visual art (painting, sculpture, drawing and also fabrics).

So I worked there for quite a long, long time. Mount Hampden. That's in Harare. Mt. Hampden Youth training center. It's in Northwoods, that's where we had that training center, ex-combatants now. Where people, after the war, came and learned new skills to integrate them into the new society.

I was there nearly six to seven years, then there were a couple of frustrations at the end. I had anticipated that the music department be really developed into a very viable, strong thing, but it was always more money, more money, more money, and I really got frustrated. I then left and formed another organization called Chipawo (Children's Performing Arts Workshop). We started this with the three of us, that's myself, Dr. Robert McLaren, and Steven. I was responsible for music and Dr. Robert McLaren was responsible for drama, for theatre. Steven Chifunyise was responsible for dance.

This was just a small group—teaching, because we realized that when developed countries provide aid to Zimbabwe, and some of these other African countries, they always think of the rural child, they look at the rural community or the rural child as sort of underdeveloped. But they forget to realize that in the urban areas there are also children that are culturally undeveloped. On Saturdays and weekends they have nothing to do, they just roam around on the roads, and day after day they are losing these cultural things. And we said, we have to look for a grant and address this issue and have workshops for the urban children. So we then embarked on CHIPAWO. It's still running, but now it developed into a very big, big, big organization.

So it now has grown and we've recruited some young people to come and teach, and I occasionally visit them to see if they are still on course and just to adjust things. I think they are on course. That is as far as that project is concerned. Also I started to build marimbas. I used my theory to help me build instruments. I had to start from building instruments, but now I have a backyard workshop which mostly people from Japan have visited, and also some from North America, many, many people. They think that this backyard type of a thing is fully equipped, but it's not! It's the traditional adze and chisel, and no machinery! Maybe it's just the drill.

Most of the work is done by hand, and also we use that backyard thing to train other people, locals and foreigners to come build marimbas. Also, I've trained some people in CHIPAWO to build marimbas and there is what they call the Research Development Center. They came to find out how to build marimbas, just in this backyard again. So it has seen many, many people. And a lot of people have learned to build marimbas just working around the backyard.

MC: So I'm sure Claire Jones came there, didn't she?

FG: Yea, she knows the backyard, she has a couple of photographs of the backyard. Then also I had to keep myself a little bit satisfied on the other end. We had to form what we called Marari Marimba Ensemble, made up of adults and married people. We play for weddings and gigs and other things like that. I have been working with that group. The most interesting thing about Marari Marimba is that 1) we do not have a leader, 2) we give; like if you're learning a song, we just come together, we say this is the "basic," the tune, this is the melody. Basically it goes like this, but the rest of the musical stuff, you have to put it together, create something. So that's basically what it is, then I also teach at Groombridge Primary School and also at a German school as a part-time teacher, and also sometimes people come and consult with me, and we've done a CD with another marimba.

MC: That's a lot. That's a lot of things that you've done, and are doing. You keep quite busy. How often do you get out of the country and come to things like here now? Are you on a tour here now?

FG: Yes, it's once in a year. That's when I come out to—out of the country, to Europe or to North America, when they have their summer. That's when I come here and work along these lines. When I finish this one, I go back home.

MC: Do you have one planned for next summer? Over here, or to Europe?

FG: No. The reason why I was keen to come is that we are planning to have Zimfest 2003 in Zimbabwe. It's like my coming here year after year successively is now to sensitize them to start to get a feel and align me with things. To align things so that if there are questions, when we have discussions then those questions asked directly are responded to.

MC: I noticed in some of the feedback after the festival last year that there were some people that were uncomfortable with things that were going on. That came out in that kind of town meeting and in some of the e-mail things later. Do you think that the Festival is going in the right direction, in your opinion? And when/if it comes to Harare next year or the year after, do you think that it would turn a different direction?

FG: Yes. Why I suggested having it in Zimbabwe, is that we are looking at it basically from two ways: 1) For the good of the people in Zimbabwe, and 2) At the same time also for the good of all people that play Zimbabwean music—American, Asia, Australia. We'll be inviting these people so that they have a better insight of exactly what it is on the ground. Sometimes there is a bit of danger in that you find that foreigners playing the Zimbabwean music, they've never been to Zimbabwe. Sometimes their mental or psychological impressions are not correct. And so by way of having that sort of a festival in Zimbabwe, I think it enlightens the people that are interested in Zimbabwean music. On the other hand, also a lot of Zimbabweans, who are much better teachers than ourselves, somehow may not be able, they have no connections, they have no links to these things, to what is going on outside Zimbabwe. By these other people visiting down there in Zimbabwe, it then simplifies and makes things easier. Then that way they may also get contact.

MC: I think it's a great idea. It makes a lot of sense. Wouldn't the ideal be that every other year you could do it that way. One year out of the country and then back in Zimbabwe and then back, so you're constantly going back to the home of the music.

FG: Um...we also have to consider costs.

MC: It's not realistic, is it?

FG: Yes. The idea itself would be good, but the logistics and the costs would be prohibitive. But once in ten years...

MC: I should be careful how I ask this question. I haven't been involved in the Festival very much. I attended one in Seattle probably about five years ago, four or five years ago. I just attended part of it, and then I read what comes on Dandemutande so I kind of know what's going on. I attended once in Canada, then the one in Eugene and now this one, and I have some impressions. I was lucky enough to get to go to London, to their Zimbabwe Music Festival, Kusanganisa. I don't know if you're familiar with that one? *(I asked if Farai knew about the Zimbabwe Music Festival in London, Kusanganisa; he did not)*

I was really impressed with that one because of the more broad areas of expertise, even academic areas that were brought together there. Not just the performing of the music or the learning to play the mbira and marimbas and the hoshos and dance, but it was more tying in to the whole culture. Even things related, for example, certainly visual arts were a part of it, film—there was a session on film. I know film is not so big in Zimbabwe, so they were pushing geographically outside of Zimbabwe. There were some films from North Africa where they're making more films. And there was a very interesting session on religion. A person of the Shona religion, a Druid from Great Britain, and an African American Baptist and they did a session talking about religion in those three different settings...very interesting!

FG: Very interesting! It's like this Zimbabwean thing we are looking at, after my experience meeting at the last Zimbabwean Festival, which I pointed out in my report, there are things that we have to begin now to think, given this modern world, what it is today. There are many things, there are other very important things that are related to any cultural development of any nation. Those things are left out and are not taken care of. They might sound academic and there is this reluctance. As far as I can see, some, when it comes to the academic side, when we discuss the issues, they are sort of reluctant.

Some of them try to cover themselves by using blankets, the spirit, the spirit, and the spirit. Now I think even in Zimbabwe, that is virtually going away. We are now confronting the music. We are now working with the culture in the context of the world today. Another thing that is here, something that personally I would like to see, when we have the Zimbabwe Music Festival, is how do I bridge tradition and technology?

How do I bridge tradition and technology so that you get the best out of it. It's an issue that most of the festivals that I've gone to have never addressed. But their musicians, their performers, their teachers are constantly being pushed forward by technology. There are microphones, today we're using computers. There are a lot of things that need to be revisited. When we have this Zimbabwe Music Festival, we'll look into all those broader academic issues. Rather than just, can you teach me one line of marimba? Can you teach me tenor part? The cultural exchange is not broad enough sometimes—it's shallow. It can be deeper. But I think we have to persuade some of the people to start thinking along those lines.

MC: I think that the learning to play the instruments, even if it's just part of a song, or a whole song or whatever, that's kind of the hook into it, and then you have to start doing more in-depth. I totally agree with you. Just a few more questions. I'll give you a chance to say whatever you want to at the end. Do you have a story or an incident that stands out as one of your worst moments, like one of your worst performances? Something funny happened, or something really terrible? And then maybe a real high moment—your best, something that was wonderful that happened—special?

FG: Ok. Well, not really tragic or the worst thing, but what I've been thinking about was the other day when our group had been invited to go and play for a very important occasion, and these guys that had invited us just kept on saying, is everything ok? We were always saying everything is fine. Then we picked up marimbas, we went to this place, and now we discovered that we forgot the bag of the playing sticks! And we discovered that we'd left them just five minutes before. And this guy was always warning us, is everything ok? We said, no, don't worry about anything. So it was now very difficult for us to go back and tell him that. But somehow that is the thing that happened. We forgot that. We had to send someone—we found someone at home to quickly bring those sticks and they were there in about 45 minutes.

MC: What did you do for forty-five minutes?

FG: We were just looking at each other (all laugh heartily). We were just looking at each other. We were so shy even to move around the people. We just looked for a small place and sat there quietly and this guy who was asking is everything ok, was looking up and down, and we were just like....(laughs!) That's something that really happened to me. I will never forget about that, no! Someone checking on you for a week, then you mess it up on the LAST five minutes!! Everybody talks about this, so since that time every member of the group notices the sticks. Where are the sticks? We can't repeat it. So that's really one of the things—we had to formally apologize. We had to formally apologize to the people, so they say, ok, don't worry, but next time, please be sure that you remember the sticks.

MC: So now when you think back can you think of a real high, high moment? One of your best?

FG: One of my best. This is difficult to tell which one is best, but one of the best times was something very encouraging in my life. I think one of the best and most encouraging things in my life was an offer to come to North America. I'd been to Europe, I'd been to Australia, and I think I have an idea of which way African music, especially Zimbabwean music in context, is going. I personally am very, very happy with the way the people that invited me to come are working. There are no meets or stories, or instructions to do this, don't do that, do this, this is better like this, if you do it like this the spirits will be angry, or anything like that. I had heard that many, many, years ago that there were many, many stories, many beliefs, and people saying I don't know what it means? What Zimbabwean music is all about. So I was saying to myself, if I could get a chance of going to North America it would be good. So when it came it was like a relief. When I came last year it was partly just to make sure, is it true what I hear? It came to be true, what I had heard when I was in Zimbabwe. So it's been very confirmed in my mind that this is true. Each time when you have your workshops you're also battling to overcome some of the incredible beliefs, that even in Zimbabwe, we've never heard about such things. But some people here in North America, they just dip their heads into it so deep that sometimes you are also frightened as a teacher.

That if it is this deep, then it's an issue that you have to address over a long, long period. And I think if also the people are able to come to the Zimfest in Zimbabwe, it might also help a lot. Sometimes the music is approached with a reverence to such an extent that we say, hmm, this is not it, this is not it.

MC: I appreciate you speaking out on that and I think it was your e-mail that impressed me that here was somebody who was saying something that probably needed to be heard. Needed to be said, needed to be heard. Farai stated it well, I thought. I did not have full enough understanding myself, but I also understood and appreciated that you were being very careful not to say anything negative because you like the fact that they want the music, and want to get into it and understand it and play it. But that there's more.

FG: To it...yes.

Grayson Capp: A lot of emotion but without understanding.

FG: Yes, without understanding. And we have that type of a situation. You as a teacher, you are confronted with this, yet at the same time, you want to develop the enthusiasm, the interest. On the other hand, trying to reveal the truth, and sometimes the truth, you can see it if I say it right now, I may do more harm. Sometimes you withdraw until you see that proper space. I think we now are at ease with each other—we can talk. But it takes a long time, so it's that conflict

GC: You realize you don't know even though you have lived in Zimbabwe two times.

FG: Yea, that's it. It's like, taking my daughter, just as an example, when you say to her, United States of America, she thinks of Disneyland. She thinks that you sit down, I press a button, the coffee comes, or I press a button, I go to the bedroom, I sleep. If I want to say, do that. Each time she was saying to me, Dad, "How are they living when you were there; I think you were having a wonderful time, you don't have to worry about anything. If you have to go anywhere you just do something (laughs). That's what the trouble is. People are people anywhere.

(I asked if it would be different doing this interview at Farai's home in Harare)

FG: I don't know really, but I think here we are not personalizing things; we are looking at this cultural education. It's just something we are looking at. What we are doing is sharing some of the concepts and concerns, and also negative concerns, so personally we are "at home" here, and we just look at it in that context.

MC: I must say, for me personally, to be in Joyce Makwenda's home or to be in Stella's home, or Oliver's or Bryan Paul's, all these musicians, I feel like I understand them in a different way, a better way, because I was in their homes. In some cases even met some other family members. Do you have anything you want to add before we quit, that you might have left out, like your dream for the future? I've asked some of the others what is their dream for the next five years, or for the next period in your life. Do you have something?

FG: Yes, this is what I would like to see in my dream. It's always been with me for many, many years. It is to see a Music Education Center in Harare. Yes, we have those places, but I think it is to have a new music center in Harare where we take another dimension into music, because music is not only about entertainment. It's deeper than that. Focusing on the children. Where we use music also, for entertainment, that's ok, but also a sort of healing area, that area has never been developed, music therapy. It's for only people who have needs beyond the entertainment part of it. But I think we need now to begin to look also into that. And also of greater concern, we are setting up this music center in which we've emphasized the teacher.

The person who shall be teaching this, so it would be a center mostly to train and educate music educators into today's world, so that when they leave that center with its own unique curriculum, they then go back to the children, with a broader perspective, where you can use music for many, many, many things. You can open up music to every child. You don't need a talented child to be in music to do a music project. You can integrate music with other things for example, to integrate music with theatre, with dance, with other subjects, e.g. sciences. When the science teacher is talking about the acoustics of sound, you as a music teacher can integrate science into this lesson. That way the other people will see the integrated approach of life. What we have now, music learning is detached from other parts of life. Now music is an afternoon activity. That is the approach at the moment. What impression does that give to the children at school? At the Center, in my dream, it will be integrated.

(I mentioned the new link between the Zimbabwe College of Music and the University of London, which has been formalized)

MC: The idea is that people can come down from London, researchers want to come down from the UK and study things that are going on in Zimbabwe, music things. And, at the College of Music they want to be able to send some of their teachers, like a violin teacher, back to London to get some more training, and so that's the way it might work. A mutual kind of thing, but what I hear you saying is something that would come on a different level, but it seems to me it's in their goals as well. Do you think that they could do it if they were to think more like you're suggesting, that's it's possible that the University of Zimbabwe, the College of Music, and the University of London could unite to do what you're suggesting?

FG: The problem there is—this is my own way of looking at it. It's not everyone else's but it's the way I look at the Zimbabwe College of Music...you have to consider its historical background. If the foundation is square, right? Whatever is to be put on that foundation has to be relatively the same shape. So if you want them to make other shapes up there you may have a crack; then there's this thing that little bit worries me. And I know some of their graduates come from there. I'm not blaming anyone, but I have a lot of questions, when you look at the modern child today. I ...hmm hmm. I have a lot of questions.

(I asked if the Zimbabwe College of Music, traditionally a conservatory, can embrace Ethnomusicology?)

FG: This is a big question. How do you bring in tradition and technology ? I think the possibilities are there, if you have the right people! If you have the right people from both ends, who are prepared, then I can see a possibility.

LUCKY MOYO

Several years ago, a friend invited me to go hear and see Black Umfolosi, a music and dance group from Zimbabwe, perform at Seattle Center. I went and was rewarded with a wonderfully energetic and inspiring performance. They were polished and very professional, but retained much of the spontaneity and freshness of traditional Zimbabwean music. Lucky Moyo was a member of that group, I found out later. I saw that same energy and excitement when I briefly observed a Zulu dance class taught by Lucky at the Zimbabwe Music Festival in July, 2002 at Seattle Center. I talked with Lucky at the Festival, and he told me that he is now living in the U.K. and working for a charitable organization there. He enjoys his work with kids, and hopes to bring his own three children from Zimbabwe to the U.K. soon.

In the interview, Lucky told me that, even though he was a student at Cambridge in the U.K., he could not read or write music. It was a keen reminder that Zimbabweans raised in rural villages, or even in urban areas, do not find it easy to become musically literate, even in a very literate university environment. For rural blacks, much of their learning is aural traditionally, even though the colonial system did provide for some education in literacy, but not necessarily in music literacy. Lucky's English was excellent and he was unusually articulate. Obviously reading and writing music was not a requisite for his musical career. Because Lucky grew up in southern Zimbabwe, his musical influences came from Botswana and South Africa as well as Zimbabwe. For him singing, drums and dance were the important influences, not mbira and marimba. He reminded me of the fact that certain drums were only played by certain people because they were sacred and special. Vocal and dance coaching and teaching, both individual and group, using a collaborative approach, are what Lucky enjoys doing, when he is not performing. His method of imaging, or "audiating" (thinking and hearing internally), creative musical compositions in his head, brings to mind the work of Edward Gordon, in music education in the U.S.

For the musical group with which he is affiliated, Black Umfolosi, Lucky stressed the importance of making the songs fit, and communicate with, the particular audience. Because of his many years of experience in this well-known and highly respected group, he talked of issues relevant to performance, including music technology, improvisation, audience behaviors, and so on. Lucky's philosophy of music making and performance is inclusive, in that he believes that performing traditional music, as well as mixtures, or fusion, is the best choice. Lucky finds Nelson Mandela to be a strong role model for African leaders and for any African person. Mandela understood simple people, and he danced, clearly something that appealed to Lucky.

Myrna Capp: I'll give you an idea of the kinds of questions I'll be asking and we'll start out with just one. Where you were from originally, where you were born, your early environment in your home, were your parents musical, your family musical, your early schooling—just all the influences that were around you when you were growing up. Here you are at Cambridge University in the U.K., a very literate place!

LM: I still can't read or write music.

MC We'll just start out with, where are you from?

LM: I'm from the west part, southwestern part of Zimbabwe, Rountree, which is a very small border town next to Botswana. It's an area where lives the Kalanga people, a very small group of people. Maybe there are more of them in Botswana. I grew up there and went to school there, primary school. There's always been music within those communities because we have one big ceremony, apart from the small evenings where people gather for beer festivals, or beer drinking fundraising. We have a festival where people go and pray for the rain, and once the rains come, people go and give thanksgiving ceremonies, to a place that we call gamari, a place of worship. So there's lots of music, singing, drumming and dancing. It's something that I grew up with. We sing a lot.

MC: Playing instruments and singing, both?

LM: I think it was more singing and dancing than playing instruments. It was only late that I started playing around with drums. Of course some of the drums were ceremonial drums and we were not allowed to play them. We only played them once we were grown up. So I started playing drums at school, not at home.

MC: Why weren't you allowed to play them?

LM: Because they were ceremonial drums, and they were really special, so we couldn't play around with ceremonial drums, because they were sacred. But also I think we would just mishandle them.

MC: Uh-huh, as kids do.

LM: They might pour some water on them, or something. Yes, that wouldn't be nice.

MC: You mentioned in your Workshop, which I attended at the Zimbabwe Music Festival, the tribes that your parents are from, and I wondered if you want to say any more about that?

LM: I think just growing up in a place where I was, Kalanga and Ndebele, those are the two languages, and the two cultures mixing, really helped me, because I grew up speaking both languages. Also, I was being exposed to the two traditions, and eventually, of course, quite a lot of music of South Africa, because my father used to work in South Africa. So he would come back with a lot of music from South Africa and then play that every time. Normally if somebody was working in South Africa at that time, they were regarded as really special because they used to get more money than the people who worked in Zimbabwe. And so anything that they brought home was sort of fashionable, so he would play music, and these visitors would come and see him. I asked him more for that music.

MC: Is that phenomena still alive, that there's a lot of respect, and kind of awe for things coming in from South Africa?

LM: Oh, yea, yea! South Africa has always been regarded as superior in terms of jobs, in terms of image, in terms of resources, in terms of quite a lot of other things. That still exists. I think if you put on a pair of trousers, people think, "Is that from South Africa?" before they even ask if it's from England or from Germany or elsewhere.

MC: Does this have any negative effect? Is that a problem for some of the music traditions in Zimbabwe, some influences from South Africa, and therefore Western influences?

LM: I think it's a problem for local musicians. People tend to like music from South Africa and from the UK and America. Then a lot of the traditional or local music is not played or is made to feel, or be considered a bit inferior. But having said that, I think on the other hand, it's good, in that people like us can say, if those guys can do it,

let's start working seriously and be able to do it. So we use that as a measure of achievement that we can compete against.

MC: So there's positive in it too. When you were in school, do you want to talk about what was going on there, musically?

LM: Yea, school music was just like another extra curricular activity, it wasn't a main subject at all. But having said that, I think because everyone came from there, we would sing ceremonial songs or even church songs. We have a church called Zion Christian Church, and this church involved people singing and dancing and doing things. Also our services, I mean every day meant singing in the morning and then prayers, singing and then prayers, and I think quite a lot of our singing in tune, came out of that background.

MC: So was it a Christian school?

LM: Well, yea, I think Christian tends to be the official religion. Like they play Christian songs, but within the school we have quite a few denominations, and we have people worshiping who also come from some different religions. It was just a government school, a public school.

MC: Can you talk about when you decided that music was something you were going to do for a profession? How did that happen?

LM: What happened was, we formed this group at school and we were all young boys singing just for the fun and the joy of doing it. It turned that our teachers got involved and they asked us to perform for some "Open Day" and welcome visitors to our school, and eventually we started being invited to such events like Trade Fairs and other national events. Then when performing at this one Trade Fair a guy from Swaziland came across us and he invited us to Swaziland and suddenly, that was 1987, and we were in a plane and going to Swaziland. It was my first time on a plane! And when we came back, we had our teachers and everyone thinking that maybe we should continue. We started getting engagements and were on television a great deal. But we didn't have any intentions of doing that. In 1990 we were invited to go to Scotland to some shows there, and then we came across this agent who wanted us to come back to England again, and Australia. From that time it's just gone on to build up. I don't know how it's been happening but it's been building up and building up, but now we realize we probably need to keep building it up more, and therefore we are now beginning to do things on the management and technical as well as artistic side.

MC: Now when you first started out, a bunch of high school boys, kids, you weren't called Black Umfolosi then, were you?

LM: Oh we were called Black Umfolosi, we named ourselves Black Umfolosi I think, maybe a week after we started. Black Umfolosi is the name of a river in South Africa. Yea, there's two rivers, there's White Umfolosi and Black Umfolosi River, and we named ourselves Black Umfolosi River. And now there's another group of young people called the White Umfolosi group. It's a group that we work with as well.

MC: Black Umfolosi was in Seattle, and I went with Natalie Kreutzer. It must have been like eight years ago or so, and I heard you in Seattle and was very impressed with the dancing and the music. It all worked together beautifully. Let's talk about more specifics about the music. Do you write songs or do you compose songs? Say you want a new song for your group, how does it happen?

LM: The way we do it is, everybody composes in the group. All the members compose and this way we think we have an advantage doing that, because we have different influences. We have some people who do religious songs, some do love songs, romance, some do political songs, some do social issues, and like I'm saying, then we can all contribute because our creativity is diverse. But we've got some songs that are traditional, that we tend to sing, because we would like them to be passed on from generation to generation. And then we've got some other songs, songs about particular events and composed for special occasions, that we sing as well. But ordinarily we write our own songs.

We work fulltime in the arts. We look at ourselves as people who are just as good as people that work for Mercedes Benz or IBM. So we wake up in the morning thinking we've got to work. It's like everybody else going to the commuter transport, e.g., bus, train and so on. That approach has helped us and helped quite a lot of other young people as well. If somebody's having a wedding and they want us to perform at their wedding, we do a special song for that wedding, that event, so that they feel that we've made it really special for each person. We've got four CD's out now.

MC: How about when you play some songs from your CD, and you change it and it's not the same as on your CD? What do audiences think? Do they want it to be exactly the same as it is on the CD?

LM: When we play, like I'm saying, our show changes. We still play a song maybe the same way, same everything. The lead singer, for instance, might play around with where we are. Like for instance, if we are singing a song that Bulawayo boys play, and we come to Monterey California and say, "Monterey boys or Monterey people, can you hear this song and make it yours?" We customize the songs to the location where they are performing. We make our show fit and *interrupt with, or customize it to* wherever we are, so that through music, we are talking and communicating, rather than just a performance; it's communal. It's fun. We're doing it on stage, but we must make sure that the other people, we don't perform for them, we perform for ourselves and to ourselves, and then to them. Then the interactive thing, we're together.

MC: When you teach do you teach mostly groups, or do you do some one to one teaching?

LM: Both. There are times where we would work as a group and teach groups. And at times if somebody wants to do some work with their voice, and they want some vocal techniques, then I spend time with them on the vocabulary, and then the sound and the tone, how they produce particular sounds. This is how I do quite a lot of work. Lately I've been doing quite a lot of work on the arrangement side, with groups, as opposed to just the artistic side. Like helping them set up things. Some groups have problems, and they are wondering how they could approach those problems.

MC: As I think back on the musicians I have interviewed, I don't think any of them teach dance. I'm really curious. What's the hard thing about teaching dance, or what's the most fun about teaching dance?

LM: Gosh, the hard thing, I don't know. I can't think of any hard thing as long as I know the dance myself. But the fun thing about this is that within the process of dancing, people make mistakes and their mistakes can actually be a good one that you could incorporate. I found that even within the singing, at times you sing with people and they go like (Lucky sings), and you find that what he sings is really nice. And then you find out that--let's go this way, and then you go with them, and then that also makes that person feel comfortable. If they make a mistake and you go (Lucky yells, "Oh no!!") then they're really afraid and then they don't keep trying. If they can make a mistake and you find that it's a good one, take it, and say, "No matter, we do it this way...take this," then that's facilitative.

MC: I like that, because as a classical pianist I always had to play exactly what's on the page, you know? The way Bach did it, the way Beethoven wanted it, and then I took a little bit of jazz and they said, you know, your mistakes could be some of your best.

LM: Yea, I think we tend to do that. When we do our show, we're playing and the audience is having a good time. My line is normally (he sings). I could (Lucky sings again with some changes to the melody to demonstrate his point) play around, and then immediately go back, and the musicians in the group, or the audience? go, "What, why did you do that?"

MC: Do you practice just yourself, by yourself?

LM: Yea, before the show we normally sing something together as a team, or do prayers, but then I normally go (he sings) with my voice. I normally rehearse with my voice. It goes from deep bass all the way into soprano. I have a voice that I can play around with.

MC: Could you demonstrate your range?

LM: Yea. I could go, let me say I'm singing maybe (he names a song) which is a special song dedicated to my Mom and Dad (he sings a phrase in the bass range, then baritone, then tenor, then alto, and soprano). So I could go to all these voice ranges or combined voices, three part, four part, maybe five, six, seven parts, or however many parts you want.

MC: Great range you have!

LM: Yea.

MC: Have you studied any Western music theory at all, I mean scales, chords and all that?

LM: No, I've not done that at all. I've been to one workshop where they covered quavers and crotchets (quarter and eighth notes) and other things, but I can't remember what quavers and crotchets are, you know? I thought it was fine, but like I'm saying, for me music flows, the words just keep flowing. I start off with the words and harmonies. I start off with the harmony and then go into the words. It depends on the occasion, but I could be here in class, I could be in a seminar, I could be really concentrating in a seminar, but at the same time I am composing and writing. A melody, or those words coming back to me again and again.

MC: Impressive! Would you say, in performances you feel really relaxed? I mean, you're not uptight about them?

LM: No, it could be 5,000, 50,000 people in a stadium. I will just be having my tea before I go onto the stage, and I feel exactly the same as if I were performing for five people. I just feel real relaxed and enjoy it myself, and once I enjoy it, I think the other people will just get that image and connect at the same level.

MC: Is that probably true for most people in Black Umfolosi?

LM: Oh yea. I don't find that when we get to a big audience, we panic or mess up our act. We just go and sing and enjoy it and then relax and the audience does too.

MC: That comes from all those years, doesn't it, of being together, and just knowing how to think together?

LM: Yea. I find that working together all these years now, at times it means that, we just don't perform the song because we know it, we perform it distinctively, perform it in the moment. I could sing the song, it takes me away from the stage and when the guy who calls for us to dance, and says, "Dance," I find I go in to the dance, but my mind is actually away. And then suddenly it comes back, and then I go, "Oh, I went away there," and then it's my mind now, in the system, in the performance.

What happens is we get into places, we tend to want to study the audience. When we go for the first song, (he sings) we try to communicate with them, and tell if they are with us. Then we try and get them to go along with things, but we have to play along with them sometimes. We get a very enthusiastic audience and then find that we want to keep going on and on and on. But now, they're clapping and clapping and they go really fast. Then we go (he sings slowly, to slow things down). But we do like to communicate--like they're going fast, and then they slow down, but we always start with them at the level where we think we should. Because, for instance, when we deal with young people, in a primary school, they're very different from an elderly audience in a public theatre. First of all, it's very different from a theatre, the setting, so we tend to adjust depending on the environment.

MC: Do you find that your audiences really want and need a beat? Or is that something that's a part of most everything you do? What about that whole idea of a beat?

LM: I find that it depends where we are, when we are in Zimbabwe. Because when you sing in Zimbabwe, and you try and do it, people just come on the stage, and some of them come and they sing much better than us. But if we are here in the States, you find that a lot of times people are so scared to come on stage because they feel that everyone will observe them and rush them. But having said that, if we perform and really don't get people grooving to things, then they feel, they say, you didn't get us to give more. You should have got us to give more. Yea, they want to get involved, participate!

MC: How important is it to you to be open to the music of other cultures? You know, Latino, music of Asia, whatever? Does your group give any thought to that or are you pretty much having to focus just on music of Africa?

LM: I think we are mixed. We've got some members who think we should just be focused on our music and Zimbabwean traditions. But then we've got some members, including myself, who think that, even in Ireland, it is surrounded by water, so if it's an island, there must be some way that makes it an island. It's surrounded by water. There is nothing that can exist in isolation, and music cannot exist in isolation. Also as the world moves, as people move, as everything just goes, you know, with technology, with cars, with everything, that the arts are not any different. I was saying to somebody that it's in almost the same way that doctors are exchanging ideas about diseases there and there, in almost the same way car manufacturers are saying where their Nissan headquarters are at Santa Cruz. But their products are in Korea and South Africa and everywhere. Musicians should be saying, "Mbira music, it came from Zimbabwe, but it's all over the world." This music came from there, there, and so on. We should mix and mingle. It's music that brings people together in an informal, leisurely, relaxed atmosphere.

MC: Here we are in California and we're focusing pretty much on the music of Zimbabwe. Do you think we should be paying a little bit of attention to some music from around here, Latino music, or something?

LM: Oh yea. I mean people have choices, and normally you always have your favorite type of shoe or favorite T-shirt and this and that. I think the more one listens to music from all over the world, definitely the more you find that you grow by understanding those cultures, maybe reading sleeve notes or just listening to the music. If you are somebody who is aspiring, and doing music, the more you listen to different styles and different types it helps with rhythm, with style, and with everything. And also, I believe that music communicates where words don't communicate, and where we get the language barriers, and the word barriers.

MC: Can you think of one of your worst moments that you've had in performance or as a musician?

LM: Let me see. I think, if anything, the worst moment, if you go to a venue, maybe you've got some elderly people who are not taken care of, maybe it's to do with my background. Or maybe you've got somebody in a wheelchair and they want to come up front and no one is there. Going off stage to go and grab that person and get them to come up front, because it's that thing about access.

I don't really have any big nightmares. I mean they are small issues that normally happen. Or we get to a venue where the microphones are just poorly organized, and things like that. It's more an issue of efficiency than anything else, and if I worried with it, normally I would go on stage frustrated, because the stage is somewhere where one should go really happy, and really enjoy themselves.

But then at big moments and big times, my God, there are so many of them. I think, one of them was when we went to perform for Nelson Mandela. I've met great people because of music and every person that I've met, I keep saying this to even children in primary schools, that the children are also great people in their own way, because every person is great in their own way. Some will be great, because you've shaken hands with somebody who's got more money, shaken hands with somebody who is politically important, somebody who's fought for human rights. But I think there are positive moments every day. Just to think that I can sing and relax and enjoy it.

MC: *(We talked about Nelson Mandela)* He's an amazing man.

LM: Mandela. You think that, when he got out of prison he could have shown all the other African leaders. "Say you guys, you just go there for internment." These African leaders just go there for one term, serve, and then come out, but he didn't. And also you think that he was a leader who really understood simple people. You could see Mandela dancing to music. He's good at this, that he could do a dance, and for me, I think that's why I could be anything today. I could be a leader, I could be a politician, I could be anything. I am a human being.

MC: What's your dream? Do you have a dream for the future for you?

LM: My big dream is...I don't really want to make a lot of money. But if I had the opportunity to make any big monies, or to be big, or the group was to be big, I would like to do some work with communities back home. Like go back to my primary school and build a library for them, and maybe go to another part of the world, do a big show and put all proceeds to some really good cause, inspire the local people to do the same. I wish I could work for charity. If somebody can cover my salary and I could just work--just raise money for good causes, then I think I would feel really, really fulfilled. Personally, I have a house, I have a car, in not so good condition. I've got things a lot of my friends don't have, and so when I look at them I feel like I've done something. I could maybe do more, but now I'd like to do things for my community.

va, 1999

Mana Pools, 1999

Acknowledgements

This book has been shaped by many people who have spent long hours bringing it to fruition. I thank each of the musicians for their openness and generosity in sharing their stories with the world. They are the heart of the project. Special thanks are due Kristin Capp for her contribution as photographer, and providing overall support and encouragement at all levels. The expertise of Grayson Capp, my husband, and Teri Capp, was especially valuable. I am grateful to Chris Timbe, Claire Jones, Ralph Gibson, Robert Lyons, Ed Marquand, Katie Donahue and Washington Lawyers for the Arts for their help.

I am grateful to Chris Waterman, Barbara Lundquist, Ephat Mujuru, and Dumisani Maraire. Thanks to Jennifer Burch, Janet Miller, W.C. Nyaho, Joan Capp, Natalie Kreutzer, Patricia Campbell, Kenneth Schubert, John Wiley, Marilyn Kolodzieczyk, Debbie Metcalfe, Delbert Miller, Laura Arksey, Irene Staunton, Ellen Koskoff, Timothy Madigan, Loran Olsen, Andrew Tracey and Horace Boyer. Thanks are also due to Seattle Pacific University for an initial seed grant that helped initiate this project. I thank Evelyn Youngren, my mother, for her continuing interest and support through the years.